BEST SERVED COLD

Akintunde Akinkunmi

AMVPS

Published by

AMV Publishing

P.O. Box 661
Princeton, NJ 08542-0661
Tel: 609 2270220; Fax: 609-7164770
emails: publisher@amvpublishingservices.com &
customerservice@amvpublishingservices.com
worldwide web.amvpublishingservices.com

Best Served Cold
Copyright © 2017 Akintunde Akinkunmi

All rights reserved. No part of this publication may be reproduced, stored in a retrieval system, or transmitted in any form or by any means, electronic, mechanical, photocopying, recording or otherwise without the written permission of the publisher.

Book & Cover Design: AMV Origination & Design Division

Library of Congress Control Number: 2016917618

ISBN: 978-0-9984796-0-6

DEDICATION

For Folusho, Kemi, Toyin & Tosin…my Ogas at the Top

PROLOGUE

Manhattan, New York

Mike was struck by how flat he felt. It felt like the burning passion, which had driven him up to this point, had burnt out, and was spending itself in the most unlikely setting of this Federal Courthouse. He barely took in the cold, impersonal feel of his surroundings — the functional, typically uncomfortable government-issue furniture, the unimaginative attempts at decoration, the muted hum of the air-conditioning that struggled to keep out the heat of New York in August. He found it strangely difficult to focus on the man whom he had pursued for so long, almost to the exclusion of everything else. When he forced himself to do so, he thought it was funny how different he looked now. Yes, the suit and tie were sharp as always, and no doubt the shoes gleamed as they always did. Yet, there was something different, something he could not quite put his finger on. Mike thought about that for a moment, and then decided that it was the arrogant, self-assured air that had gone, replaced by uncertainty and apprehension, as they waited for the jury to return with their verdict. The defendant, Big Man, licked his lips, and frequently flicked back an immaculate cuff to glance at an expensive looking watch. Ever the showman, he tried to conceal his growing anxiety by smiling and waving at the adoring band of sycophants and hangers-on seated on the benches reserved for the public. Mike idly wondered how long they would hang around for, if, as he hoped, the jury came back with a verdict that condemned their benefactor to several years as an unwilling guest of the government of the United States. He thought with a wry smile of the vicious infighting that was sure to follow over the ill-gotten millions Big Man had amassed over such a short time.

Suddenly things seemed to be moving. The law enforcement people in attendance stopped chatting to each other and took up positions around the room. The prissy, pompous court clerk bustled in, and the stenographers suddenly reappeared. The lawyers sat back at their tables, pens poised over yellow legal pads. The court rose as the judge appeared. The jury filed in and took their places. Mike scrutinized each face, hoping for a clue as to which way they would go. The foreman, a small, dark Hispanic man looked vaguely uncomfortable, as he had done since the first time Mike set eyes upon him, as if troubled by piles. Next to him was the white woman Mike had taken to calling the Bitch in his mind, although he was not quite sure why. Fatso sat next to her, looking somewhat awed by the occasion, and he actually seemed to be awake for a change. Then there was the Mad Professor, who had apparently spent the entire trial leaning forward, staring intently through his thick glasses at whomever was speaking at the time, as though he were either committing every word to memory, or divining the secrets of their souls. Mike was surprised to note that the earlier feeling of flatness had disappeared, replaced by the sort of anxiety that had accompanied waiting for exam results in his youth. Or waiting outside the labour ward all those years ago. . . He ground his teeth as he fought to suppress those memories; after all, that was why he was here to see this, wasn't it?

He glanced across at Big Man. All pretence of cool detachment had vanished. The man looked frankly terrified. His hands seemed to be shaking, and he tried to control them by firmly interlocking his fingers. He leaned over to listen to his lead lawyer, but his eyes never left the jury box. The judge ask the foreman if they had reached a verdict. "Yes, your honour, we have." The foreman passed a folded piece of paper to the clerk who handed it to the judge. The judge opened it, read what was written on it, and with no expression handed it to the clerk who cleared his throat, and in his most pompous way started to read. "On count one, we the jury find the defendant guilty. On count two, we the jury find the defendant guilty."

A low murmur spread across the room, soon drowned out by loud wailing from the public benches. Someone appeared to have collapsed. The judge was saying something about passing sentence at a later date, but Mike barely took it in. He only had eyes for Big Man, watching with a growing sense of satisfaction as the marshals handcuffed him behind his back, and led him away, a far cry from his days of pomp and importance as a senior figure in the government of his country. As Big Man disappeared, Mike noticed that it was the defendant's wife (or at least the most senior of the several wives and concubines) who had collapsed and was now being wheeled out by ambulance medics on a trolley, with an oxygen mask over her face. He felt a fleeting pang of guilt, and then remembered his own wife and children. . .

CHAPTER 1

London, England

NOT FOR THE FIRST TIME, MIKE WONDERED HOW THE hell the English managed to live with their crazy weather. It had been sleeting this morning, and now, late on this spring afternoon, the sun was going in and out of the clouds, it was freezing cold, and to top it all, hailstones the size of golf balls were falling. He half wished that he had taken his boss up on the offer of staying for one more drink at the boozy lunch they had to celebrate clinching the merger of two small companies that made feminine hygiene products, as the turgid prospectus described it. The thought of having to put up with the antics of several drunken Englishmen was enough to persuade him that it was time to cut and run. Inevitably, he would have a few himself, and become less able to put up with their prejudices which seemed to come to the fore when they'd had one drink too many, and then he might do or say something he'd regret later; no, it was better to make polite excuses and leave them to it. He toyed with the idea of going home to the swish flat in Docklands that he'd bought with last year's bonus, and maybe going for a swim, but his exercise routine did not appeal today. Perhaps he could give that pretty lawyer at the bank a call. . . now what had he done with her number?

"Why don't you bloody look where you're going?"

"I do beg your pardon, I was miles away." He smiled sheepishly at the deliveryman he'd nearly knocked off his feet, and bent to help him pick up the bundles of the evening newspaper that he'd been carrying. The man grunted an acknowledgment of the apology, and went on his way. Mike looked round and spotted one of the several coffee shops that seemed to have sprung up in London over the last few years. He'd go in for a coffee to get out of the hailstones, and have a good hunt in his wallet to find the card she'd given him earlier.

"An Americano, please."

"Sure, regular or large?" The girl behind the counter was not particularly convincing that she gave a toss either way.

"Regular's fine, thanks."

"Anything else?"

"No, that's it."

"That'll be three fifty."

Mike handed over a five-pound note and watched her search for as many fifty pence pieces as she could find in the till to give him as change. He dutifully left two of them in the saucer on the counter and took the cup from her. He wandered around, trying to find a seat, but the shop was full of other people with the same idea as him. He gave up and stood at the ledge by the window. He go this wallet out to see if he had put the lawyer's card in there, but could not find it. So much for that idea. Someone had left a copy of the same newspaper he'd just knocked over, and he glanced idly at it whilst he sipped his coffee (which was surprisingly good). He flicked through the pages of the newspaper, starting with the sports section at the back, as he usually did. Next, he glanced at the entertainment section, hoping perhaps to go and see a film. His eye was caught by an unusually large advert for a South African musical that he had seen advertised on the Tube a few days previously, and that he had made a mental note to look up—the fact that he had completely forgotten about it till now was another piece of evidence that he was getting a *little* too stressed. He saw it was on at the Barbican, which was within easy walking distance; well, that solved the problem of what to do with himself this evening. He did not know it then, but his life would take a very different course from that moment on.

There was a fairly large crowd in front of the ticket offices at the Barbican, generating a steadily increasing volume of noise. Mike took some time to work out where he needed to go to enquire about tickets, but thankfully the queue wasn't too long, and there were still tickets available, albeit at the pricier end of the scale. He bought a ticket in the stalls, as well as a glossy overpriced programme. The show wasn't due to start for another hour and a half, so he looked round for a bar to sit in and while the time away with a few drinks. The bar he found was no great shakes, but it would do. He ordered a vodka and tonic, got a bag of nuts and wandered to a table in a corner that afforded him a view of the entrance. A few minutes later, his attention was caught by a striking woman who walked in with a smug looking man dressed in jeans and a shirt that looked at least a size too small for his belly. Mike pretended to read his programme while casting an increasingly impressed eye over the woman. He would not have described her as beautiful, but there was something about her that he found attractive. He tried to decide if it was her light skin, or the way she filled out her clothes in such a sensuous way, or whether it was the haughty, somewhat arrogant look in her eyes — after some more reflections, he decided it was a combination of all three. He had just started to imagine what she would look like without her clothes on when he realised with a start that she appeared to be looking directly at him. He hurriedly averted his eyes, but not before he saw an amused half-smile play over her lips, which for some reason vaguely annoyed him. She started walking in his general direction, looking around her, and he realised she hadn't been looking at *him*; she was trying to find a free table, which annoyed him even more. She found one a few tables along to his left, and turned to wave at Beer Belly at the bar to let him know where she was sitting. For the first time, Mike turned his gaze to Beer Belly, wondering what a stunner like her was doing with someone like him. His face was pleasant enough, but with evidence of a lifestyle of too much consumption and too little exercise. He carried himself with the haughty air of one who thought quite a bit of himself. Mike thought that there was something vaguely familiar about his face as the man made his way towards the table where the girl was now sitting at, carrying a bottle of wine and two glasses. He watched him sit at the table, and pour the wine.

Mike realised he was staring, and made an effort to drag his eyes back to the programme open in his lap, but could not resist turning his eyes towards the couple every few minutes. He was surprised to note that he was now more preoccupied with trying to work out why Beer Belly's face seemed so familiar than the attractiveness of his companion. He prided himself on his memory for faces, and he just knew that he had seen that face before; it would annoy him now for the rest of the evening.

He was just starting to really wind himself up when he realised that the time had flown and it seemed that the show was about to start, as the bar, which had filled up a fair bit without his realising it, began to empty. He got up and joined the crowd heading to the theatre, but not without first casting a last glance at Beer Belly and his companion. There was something about him.

It came to him mid-way through the first session before the interval—Beer Belly had initially been a year ahead of him at school, but they had ended up graduating together after Beer Belly had been forced to repeat the third year, much to the delight of Mike and his classmates, who had suffered much at the hands of Beer Belly when he had been their senior. Although never close, he recalled that Beer Belly had been friendly enough in their last two years at school, especially as their school leaving exams approached, and the need to pass with good grades overcame any lingering feelings of animosity or superiority. Now what was his proper name?. . . Akin something or other, wasn't it? Kazeem—that was it. Niggling problem resolved, Mike turned his attention to the lithe young bodies on the stage, dancing energetically to the pulsating rhythms that only African music seemed able to generate. He could see why the show had received such good reviews—the music was superb, the set and lighting much the same, and the story line quite haunting. He settled down to enjoy the show.

"Excuse me, did you attend Sacred Heart in Lagos by any chance?"

Beer Belly turned round, with a look that suggested he was wondering what mere mortal had had the temerity to address him in this place. When he realized that the person addressing him did not seem to be in the least intimidated by the look, his expression softened a bit. "Yes, I did," he said.

"I thought so . . . Akin Kazeem, right?"

"That's right. . .you are?"

Mike stuck out a hand. "Mike Anako. . . We studied for our school cert exams together."

Recognition dawned on Beer Belly's face. "Of course! I thought your face looked familiar in the bar earlier. How are you? Long time, man."

"Indeed. I don't think I've seen you since we left school. You went off to Ife, right?"

"Correct. . . and you?"

"Stayed in Lagos to read law, and for law school, then went off to the States to do a masters, and ended up in the UK a few years afterward, been working in the City as a corporate lawyer since. What are you up to these days?"

"I'm sorry to interrupt the school reunion, but the second half of the show is about to start."

Mike was surprised that he hadn't noticed Akin's female companion, given how riveting he had found her earlier. She now added an impatient look to the previous haughtiness, which only made her look more attractive, Mike thought.

Akin looked a little sheepish. "Sorry dear, go ahead, I'll catch up with you shortly." With barely a glance at him, she swept imperiously past them without another word.

"Is that Madam?", Mike asked.

Akin cracked a somewhat knowing smile. *"For where?* She's a good friend who looks after me when I come to London, if you know what I mean"

"Say no more. Anyway, we'd better leave before you get into more trouble."

"Don't mind her *jare*. I don't know what gets into all these women that after a while they think they own you. Why don't we meet up for a drink and catch up on old times? I'm in London for a few more days." They exchanged numbers and returned to the show.

Mike was impressed, despite himself. He'd lived in London all these years and thought he knew every upper, middle and lower class dive and drinking den, but this little place off Piccadilly was a new one to him. You wouldn't have thought such discreet opulence was to be found behind the nondescript dark wood door, which had an unlabelled buzzer beside it. Mike had arrived with Akin after meeting him in the bar of the swish hotel he was staying in a couple of days after the chance encounter at the Barbican. A surprisingly pleasant meal and a few drinks, accompanied by much reminiscing about school days, followed. It was pushing midnight, and Mike was thinking about going home when Akin suggested a nightcap at this place. More out of curiosity than desire, Mike had agreed to a nightcap, but now, sitting here with an excellent brandy in his hand, in an elegantly and tastefully furnished room, he was glad he'd come.

"So how did you find this place?" Mike asked Akin.

"My boss brought me here on one of our trips to London. . . . Apparently this is where all the *Naija* Big Men in the know come, when they want to be discreetly entertained, if you get my drift."

It suddenly occurred to Mike that while Akin had said he worked 'with the government', he had not actually said what exactly it was he did, so Mike asked him now.

"I wondered when you'd ask," Akin replied. "My boss is the Minister for Business and Investment, which explains the frequent overseas trips – I am his Special Adviser on Inward Investment, which explains why I travel with him so often. It's one of the perks of the job."

"Nice work if you can get it."

Akin suddenly turned serious and leaned forward. "Have you ever thought about coming back home to Nigeria?"

"No, can't say I ever thought seriously about it. Why? Do you have a job for me?" Mike asked with a laugh.

Akin leaned back and waved a hand. An immaculately suited waiter appeared as if by magic and refilled their brandy snifters from an exquisite cut-glass decanter, and then soundlessly vanished again. When he had gone, Akin started again. "You may or may not be aware, but the present government is quite clear that it needs to divest itself of its many holdings in sectors of the economy which it believes are properly the province of private enterprise – telecoms, aviation, power, and so on. There has been a wave of privatizations, and it's not going to let up anytime soon. Many of those businesses are going to need to merge and consolidate in order to be viable. Somebody with your background and experience would be a valuable asset to us in government in terms of reassuring your *oyinbo* friends that we know what we're doing and their investments would be safe. And you could make a killing in the process. Being a special adviser to certain ministers opens doors like you would not believe."

Mike paused for a moment, taking in what Akin had said. On the face of it, it did make sense, but he wasn't quite sure if he was being pitched for a job. "So what exactly are you saying?"

"I'm saying that I could arrange an appointment for you to see my minister, and could plant the idea in his head that you would be a useful addition to the special advisers in his office."

"Really?"

Akin leaned back again with a slight hiss. "I can see you've lived abroad for too long. Do you think I would waste my time bringing you here if I wasn't serious?"

"*No vex*, it's just that I'm wondering why you would want to do this for me given that we only met again a couple of days ago after not having seen each other for more than 20 years."

"Listen, my friend, I am not a philanthropist. If you come on board and you perform, I get brownie points with the minister. If your coming in makes him shine, he gets brownie points with the president. If that happens, we all win, you included."

"Okay, point taken," Mike raised his hands. "If I'm interested, what happens next?"

"Let me have hard and soft copies of your CV before I leave on Thursday, and I'll take it from there."

"Soft copies?" Mike was puzzled.

"See, I told you. You have become an *oyinbo*. Hard copy is paper, *abi*? *Ehen* now, soft copy is electronic *na*." Mike laughed along with Akin.

"One last thing—given the amount of brandy I have drunk tonight, can I sleep on it and get back to you sometime tomorrow when I'm sober?"

"*Na you sabi.*"

CHAPTER 2

Abuja, Nigeria

MIKE COULDN'T REMEMBER THE DRIVE FROM THE airport into Abuja being quite this long before, and wondered idly, as he stared out of the window of the black Toyota SUV with government plates that had been sent to pick him up at the airport, whether it was that they were going a different way, or if his memory was playing tricks on him. On balance, he thought it was probably the latter; it had been some time, after all, since he'd been to Abuja, and some of the landmarks along the way seemed vaguely familiar. The driver and protocol officer that Akin had sent to the airport had been pretty quiet once they had whisked him from the plane exit door, through customs and immigration and into the car; a room had apparently been reserved for him at the Hilton, and he was due to see the minister later this morning before the said minister left town for his "country home" later that day for the weekend.

Things had moved fairly swiftly since Akin's trip to London a few weeks before. Mike thought to himself, not for the first time, that there was much to be said for not making decisions when pissed off. His decision to send Akin his CV had followed another crass comment from his boss at work about how much the firm valued his "African viewpoint" — whatever that meant; Mike figured he might as well explore utilizing his "African viewpoint" in Africa. His surprise at himself for sending off the CV was surpassed only by the swiftness and efficiency of the response—Akin had made contact via email within a few days to say the minister was interested, then again to offer him an interview, and finally to confirm the date and the travel arrangements and pay for them. He had arranged to take a couple of days off work (God knows they owed him enough leave), and here he was, on his way to an interview with the Minister of Business and Investment in Abuja on a Thursday. Surreal.

Having navigated their way past several checkpoints, they arrived at the hotel. It looked in somewhat better repair than Mike remembered, but this was Nigeria—things did not always seem as they appeared. He was swiftly checked in by the protocol officer, and escorted to a large room, accompanied by a large and obsequious retinue of hotel staff that appeared to have emerged from the woodwork. He assured them for the umpteenth time that he knew how the air-conditioning worked and that he should not hesitate to contact them if he needed anything and eventually managed to get rid of all of them apart from the protocol officer.

"*Oga* says that we should ensure you are at the ministry by 12 noon, so he can brief you before you meet with the minister at 1.30, so I suggest that we leave here around 11.15 a.m., sir; this Abuja traffic has been serious recently." Mike restrained himself from asking whether the Abuja traffic had previously been frivolous, and nodded agreement that he would be ready to go by then.

On his own at last, he unpacked his small carryon case and stripped off, pausing on his way into the shower to run a critical eye over this reflection in the mirror—I need to step up my exercise regime, he thought. He had a shower with tepidly warm water masquerading as cold, and returned to the relaxingly chilled atmosphere of the air-conditioned hotel bedroom. Suddenly feeling tired, he set the alarm on his phone for a couple of hours and fell asleep.

The protocol officer was right. Traffic in Abuja was not to be trifled with, and what appeared to be cars queuing for fuel at petrol stations weren't helping. They eventually arrived at the imposing building that proclaimed itself to be the Federal Ministry of Business and Investment. A fleet of black SUVs similar to the one that had picked up Mike were scattered around the compound. The protocol officer shepherded Mike through the reception procedures, and now armed with a badge carried on a lanyard around his neck that declared him to be a "Visitor- VIP", he was taken to a lift manned by a middle-aged man who looked as is he might expire of boredom any moment.

"Which floor, *sah*?"

"SSA Inward," replied the protocol officer, which Mike thought was an interesting response to a fairly simple question. The reply evidently made sense to the lift operator because he punched a couple of buttons and the lift doors closed, followed by a somewhat jerky ascent. It occurred to Mike that it was unlikely that a lift malfunction now would result in a swift or efficient rescue, and he made a mental note to himself to take the stairs next time. . . if there was a next time. The lift arrived at their destination, and they got out. Another flunky seated behind a desk greeted the protocol officer with a cheery "OC, *how far?*" and then peered suspiciously at Mike and his VIP Visitor badge before waving them both through. Protocol led him to an office on the right side of the corridor where a middle-aged female secretary sat behind a desk. Three or four others sat on chairs lining the walls. Protocol spoke to the secretary *"Oga dey? His visitor from overseas don come."*

"He went to see the Hon Minister, he said you should wait for him," she replied to Mike, ignoring the protocol guy. "Please have your seat." Mike suppressed a grin as he wondered which seat, exactly, was his, but dutifully sat down in a seat directly opposite the standing air-conditioning unit; at least he would be nice and cool there.

"Anything to drink, *sah*? Tea, coffee, or minerals?"

"I'm fine, thanks."

"Newspapers?" The secretary asked, holding out a wad of them.

"Thanks," Mike replied, accepting the papers, all stamped to say they belonged to 'The Office of the Senior Special Adviser to Hon Minister'. He dutifully browsed through the papers, and was starting to wonder how long he was going to have to wait when the door opened and Akin walked in carrying a file and talking on his mobile phone. He spotted Mike and gesticulated at him to come in to the inner office, which he did. The secretary followed Mike in, carrying several papers and shut the door behind her. Akin waved Mike to a seat in front of his vast and cluttered desk, still talking on the phone. "Yes, sir, no problem sir, I will make sure the minister sees your file before he travels . . . okay sir, no problem sir. . . alright sir, bye sir."

"Sorry I wasn't here when you arrived, the minister called an impromptu meeting that I had to go to. Hope your flight was smooth?" Akin said to Mike, adding the papers he was clutching to the clutter already on his desk.

"Fine, thanks. Nice office." Mike said, casting his eyes over the obligatory photographs of the president, the minister and the minister of state.

"Thanks, yes, what is it?" This last was directed at the still-hovering secretary.

"Sir, the perm sec's office sent up these memos for you to minute on, and finance also needs you to approve some orders. The visitors I told you about are still waiting."

"Leave the papers from the perm sec and finance, I will deal with them later. Which visitors are you talking about?"

"The ones from Alhaji Dan Kano that I told you about the other day when—"

Akin interrupted her "Did I not say they should go and see the CBN people to solve their problem?

"Sir, yes, but—"

"Madam, please don't vex me o. Let them carry their *wahala* to CBN, and if you don't take time, you will follow them too. Now get out and go and get them out of my office."

The secretary dutifully put the papers on Akin's desk and left the office.

"These people can drive you crazy if you're not careful. *Ehen, jare,* how was your trip? I hope the protocol chaps performed?" Akin returned his attention to Mike.

"I don't think I have been out of an airport quicker in my life."

"Excellent, excellent. Now, let's talk about your interview with the minister this afternoon. Did you do the presentation like I suggested?"

"Yes, I have it here."

"Good. Get it ready but don't bring it up until he asks for it. He may not do so, because he will probably want to wrap things up early before skipping town this evening for the weekend. Talking of which, if he invites you to join him for the weekend, politely decline, and plead the need to return to the UK tomorrow for work reasons—he'll be flattered to think you flew all this way just to meet with him. Last point, whatever you do, don't create the impression that you are coming to save us with the white man's knowledge of all things; the perm sec will be sitting in the meeting, and she's an obnoxious anglophobic cow, so tone down the British accent, if you possibly can—any questions?"

"Well, yes. Who else will be in this interview?"

"The minister of state is out of town, so it'll be just the

minister, the perm sec and me, as the senior special adviser. Anything else?"

"Can't think of anything."

"Great. I suggest you review your presentation once more while I clear this paperwork, then we'll go in."

In the end, it was even more straightforward than Mike had dared dream. He was in and out of the minister's office in less than half an hour, most of which was taken up by the minister's boasting about his son studying at Harvard having seen that Mike had done a master's degree in banking law at Harvard. There was a little perfunctory discussion about upcoming privatisations and the standard spiel about government working in the best interests of the people, and that, it seemed, was that. Mike would be informed 'in due course' as to the outcome of the interview — that turned out to be later that afternoon when Akin came by to pick him up at the hotel, having seen the minister off to the airport. The job, it seemed, was his, subject to 'security clearance' and the issuing of a formal letter of appointment.

The money was not great, but the job was something that he actually thought was interesting and the benefits in terms of housing, transport and travel were not at all bad. It crossed his mind as he was speaking to the partners about his wish to leave that they and others may well think him mad — who in their right mind would walk away from a well-paid job in the City of London to work as ministerial special adviser in a Third World country with no stability or job security? But leave he would, and leave he did, having arranged to rent out his flat (he could live off that alone, since he did not have a mortgage, and — best of all — as he would be living abroad, he didn't even have to pay tax). A few raucous leaving parties later, and he was leaving the grey murkiness of London behind and heading to the warm, sunny and exciting new world of Abuja. . . . What could possibly go wrong?

CHAPTER 3

Abuja, Nigeria, five years later

HOW DID I EVER LET THINGS GET THIS BAD? MIKE asked himself as he puffed and panted on the exercise bike at one of the several upmarket gyms that had sprung up in Abuja over the last couple of years, struggling to keep up with the pace being set by the disgustingly slim and fit young man who was leading this particular spinning class. The answer, of course, was that he had been captured by the myriad traps that abound in the life of a busy Big Man in Abuja — the frantic pace of running around trying to get things done, the unending tight travel schedules, the innumerable social functions all over the country (and the world) that seemed to be an integral part of doing business here, and finally, most significant of all, the fact that he was now a husband and father.

Lagos, Nigeria, four years earlier

If there was one thing about the return to Nigeria that really got up Mike's nose, it was the almost guaranteed chaos that passed for a domestic airline service. About the only thing you could be certain of was that your flight would neither leave nor arrive on time — assuming it went at all. All the other stuff he could, or had learned, to deal with, but not this. On this occasion, he was at the domestic terminal of the airport in Lagos, awaiting a flight back to Abuja, which had already been delayed by an hour, and which, according to the garbled announcement made just now with an affected *oyinbo* accent on the public address system, was now subject to a further 30 minute delay for 'operational reasons'. He was already in a foul mood from the puerile meeting he had come to Lagos to attend on the minister's behalf, which had ended with him having to apologize to the visiting French rail transport consortium who discovered, to their chagrin, that they had been stiffed by state government officials in cahoots with their Chinese competitors for a rail transit project. Mike suspected that a significant chunk of the French indignation arose from their suspicion that they had simply been out-bribed by the wily Chinese, but as the minister's representative, he had been required to pour oil on troubled waters by saying that he, Mike, would bring the matter to the urgent attention of his minister, and insinuating that his minister would have a word with his fellow minister responsible for the Federal Capital Territory to ensure that the French would be given preferred bidder status for a similar project in Abuja—God only knew how he was going to pull that one off, but it had achieved the immediate goal of pacifying the French. To then follow that with a couple of hours in the notorious Lagos traffic had been adding insult to injury... and now this. He took a deep breath and then reminded himself it could be worse. He could be sitting outside in the heat of the main departure area, rather than in the cool comfort of the air-conditioned Protocol Lounge as befitted a ministerial special adviser. The only problem was that the mobile phone signal in the lounge was poor on both his phones, so he would at some stage have to step out to call his driver waiting in Abuja to pick him up to let him know of the revised arrival time. No time like the present, so he slipped his shoes back on, picked up his phones and stood up.

"Is *Oga* leaving?"

Mike eyed the attendant balefully. Did this moron really think he would leave without his jacket and briefcase? Or had he not heard the announcement about the delayed flight? He was about to make a barbed response then caught himself — it wasn't the poor guy's fault after all, was it?

"No, I'm just stepping out briefly"

"Alright *sah*."

"So what, exactly, are the operational reasons for which you have kept us sitting in this heat for the last three hours?"

"Madam, please don't be annoyed, bear with us, the aircraft departed late from Abuja."

"Fucking cobblers."

That last, and the accent in which it was delivered, caught Mike's attention. He turned to see who it was that had used an expression he hadn't heard for a long time. His eyes alighted on a strikingly beautiful woman, dressed in a beautifully cut skirt suit, which she filled superbly in all the right places. She was about five and a half feet tall, although her heels made her look taller. Her skin was the colour of slightly milky coffee. She had an oval face, with piercing copper-coloured eyes. She wore her hair in long, fine braids, upon which were perched a pair of glasses. As he studied her, he realised she was probably about the same age as him, perhaps a bit younger and was wearing a monogrammed signet ring on her left little finger, but no wedding ring.

She turned away from the counter and caught him staring at her. Feeling a little foolish, he turned away and made the call he had come out to make in the first place. Having done so, he looked around to see where the woman who had caught his attention had gone, and spotted her on the far side of the hall, looking at the display in the window of a bookshop. She entered, and on impulse, he walked over to the bookshop as well. It really was a tiny shop, with barely enough room for more than half a dozen people, but, the half-asleep attendant aside, she was the only one in the shop.

"Pardon me, but I couldn't help overhearing your conversation with the chap at the desk just now."

She lifted her head from the book she was looking at and peered at Mike over the top of her glasses. "Really?"

"Yes, really." Mike was not going to be intimidated. "I haven't heard that expression you used in a long time."

"Well, it is fucking cobblers, the way these airlines and airports treat customers." She looked at him slightly defiantly, as though daring him to disagree with her.

"Couldn't agree more." He stuck out his hand. "Mike Anako."

Surprisingly hesitantly, given her forthrightness thus far, she shook his hand briefly. "Ronke Adesanya."

"Pleased to meet you. So, what takes you to Abuja?"

"An aeroplane, hopefully."

Mike stretched his lips in a poor simulation of a smile. "Quite. Work?"

"Yes."

"What do you do?" Mike asked. He did not want to lose contact with this outspoken woman.

"What's this – question time?"

"Another phrase I haven't heard for a long time."

She shut the book and looked at him full on. "You've got a smart answer for everything, haven't you?"

"Well, why don't you try inviting me to dinner to see whether that's true?"

Despite herself, she laughed out loud. "In your dreams! But you're good, I'll grant you that."

"I'll take that as a compliment. Now, since we're both going to be stuck here for at least the next hour, we might as well be a tad more comfortable than we are at the moment. Fancy a cold drink in the lounge?"

It turned out she was a senior executive in one of the big banks, who had relocated to Nigeria from the UK a couple of years before Mike, and was on her way to Abuja for a meeting at the Central Bank. They had apparently worked within a half-mile of each other in London. Her return to Nigeria had been the result of being head-hunted by one of the smaller banks, "an offer I'd have been daft to refuse," was how she described it—but the decision was made easier by wanting to be closer to her parents who were not getting any younger. Mike found her easy to talk to, and they chatted almost non-stop till they landed in Abuja. She declined his offer of a ride into the city (one of the bank's cars was picking her up), and his invitation to dinner (pleading the need to prepare for her meeting the next day). She did agree to exchange cards with him, and to his delight, responded in kind when he sent her a text message later that evening to say it had been nice to meet and chat with her and to wish that her meeting the next day went well.

They soon started exchanging text messages, and then phone calls on a regular basis. It took a few weeks but she eventually agreed to let him take her out to dinner. Mike soon found himself travelling regularly to Lagos to see her; in a matter of months, they had become lovers as well as increasingly close friends.

For the first time that he could remember, Mike found himself seriously contemplating the idea of getting married. He was in his mid-thirties, as was she, and whilst it was clear that neither had led a cloistered existence, they did seem to enjoy each other's company. They started going to social events together, and, inevitably, tongues started to wag.

"My friend, what are your intentions with my sister?" Akin had said to him one day.

"*Which your sister be dat?*" Mike found himself lapsing into Pidgin English at the drop of a hat these days.

"*Be asking me foolish question, you hear?* Sade is harassing me on a daily basis, mainly because she thinks you will soon start leading me astray as *you no get wife for house.*"

"If only your wife knew that you need no lessons from me in that department," Mike responded with a laugh.

"Seriously, though, what are you waiting for? It's clear that you are foolishly in love with her, and don't forget that *these women get clock wey dey tick o. Na pension you wan take pay school fees?*"

"I hear you." Mike realised with a start that the thought of children had not really crossed his mind seriously either. He wondered what his and Ronke's children would look like.

Ijebu-Ode, Nigeria, three years earlier

"You took your time, didn't you?" Ronke's father gazed at Mike over the top of his glasses — so that's where she gets that from, he thought.

"Well Sir, to be honest, I don't think either of us had thought quite this far ahead."

"You *oyinbo* children are all the same — plenty book knowledge and no commonsense. Anyway, better late than never. When are your people going to come and introduce themselves to us?"

Mike explained that his parents had died within a couple of years of each other when he and his older sister had still been young children; they had been brought up by his father's younger brother, whom he now regarded as his father. His uncle's wife had also passed away, so apart from his uncle, sister and their children, he had no other living relatives.

Ronke's Dad took this all in impassively, and Mike realised he would know all this already as Ronke would undoubtedly have shared this information with her parents, to whom she was quite close.

Mike noticed that both Ronke and her mother had made themselves scarce, leaving him alone with his future father-in-law. Bloody woman did that on purpose . . . I'm going to kill her, Mike was thinking to himself when Ronke and her Mum walked in.

"I'm impressed. You're still in one piece, and drinking Daddy's special brandy to boot. He must really like you. . . . Or is it that you're relieved that some intrepid fool has finally agreed to marry your *oniwahala* daughter?" Ronke turned to her father as she spoke these last words.

"It's not your fault," her father replied with a sigh. "I should have ignored your mother and refused to send you to school in England."

"Yeah, whatever." Ronke bent over and kissed her father's balding head. "So, what do you think about your future son-in-law?"

"Who told you I have agreed to any such thing?"

"Well, why are you sitting here drinking your special brandy with him? Who else do you share it with, apart from your partner in crime, Uncle Bunmi?" This last was her father's oldest and closest friend.

"It's called polite good manners, which clearly your expensive *oyinbo* education has done little to nurture."

"Ignore them, *joo,* my son," Ronke's Mum beamed at him. "They're as bad as each other. Anytime you need advice in managing your wife, just give me a call. I've been married to the male version of her for the last 40 years."

"Thanks Ma, I'll bear that in mind."

⌘ ⌘

Mike had been dreading the whole wedding performance — the introduction, followed by the 'engagement'/native law and custom wedding, followed, finally by the 'white' church wedding. His attempts to persuade all concerned, but especially Ronke's mum, and his own sister, that he was perfectly content to have a small registry wedding followed by a reception for a few close friends and family had been swatted aside with disdain.

Ronke was an only child, and her mum was going to make sure the world knew her only daughter was getting married.

His own sister was not going to be outdone—"We may be orphans, but your in-laws should realise that they are marrying into a family with standing in this country." And so Mike had to endure the whole nine yards.

Ronke even managed to persuade him, at one point, that he was actually enjoying it all!

He certainly enjoyed the honeymoon. After much to-ing and fro-ing, they eventually settled on a week in the Maldives, and a week in Dubai. For the first time, he and Ronke really were in each other's company 24 hours a day for several days on end, and, to their surprise they did not find it grating in the least, being content to just be around each other even when not shopping, sightseeing, having meals or making love.

What Mike really appreciated, as he told Ronke over dinner on the last night of the honeymoon, was how each was content just to let the other be, with neither of them feeling under pressure from the other. They had even agreed on their living arrangements, given that Mike's job was in Abuja and Ronke's in Lagos—they would alternate weekends to travel to each other, while Ronke sorted out a transfer to her bank's Abuja office. As it turned out, even that proved unnecessary as a major international financial consulting firm head-hunted her to set up and head their West African Regional Office in Abuja. Okay, it would require some travel along the West African Coast, and occasionally to head office in the States, but that was not that different from what she had been doing in her previous job, anyway. And she could sometimes work from home—what was not to like?

Abuja, Nigeria, one year earlier

"Mike, we need to talk." Akin poked his head round the door of Mike's office.

"Sure, come on in. Has Sade caught you again?" Mike responded with a laugh. Mike had played peacemaker between

Akin and his irate spouse on at least two occasions, when she confronted him with a number of his dalliances.

"We can't talk here. Let's meet at the guest-house, say around 9.00 p.m.? And please don't say anything to Ronke, I'll explain later."

Mike leaned back in his chair and wondered what was getting Akin so wound up. He'd looked kind of apprehensive, which was most unusual. He'd also looked serious, which was even worse. He stood up and walked over to the window overlooking the car park some six floors below, populated as usual by the fleet of black SUVs that ferried the *ogas* like him around town, and the buses which the ministry used to shuttle lower-ranking stuff to and from various points around the city. The daily 4 p.m. exodus had begun, and the staff had started swarming around the buses. The traffic around town for the next couple of hours or so would be murderous, as the scene playing out below would be repeated at several locations across town. Mike had initially taken to coming in to work early and leaving late to try and beat the traffic. Since Ronke arrived on the scene and his domestic circumstances had changed, they had moved to a very nice flat in Maitama, which made the journey to and from work a lot shorter; since Fola and Funke had arrived, the pull towards getting home earlier became even stronger.

Mike had often heard people talk about how the arrival of children could change your life; well, their twin son and daughter had certainly changed his and Ronke's lives. He still marvelled at how early on you could see the differences in their characters, and he would spend ages staring with fascination at them, even when they were asleep, much to the amusement of his mother-in-law, who'd come to stay for a few weeks to help out. Funke, older by a few minutes, was more laid back than her more raucous brother, but nonetheless both Mike and Ronke agreed that she was definitely the twin in charge;

they would beam as she would sit back and throw various toys around the room, and watch her twin brother scuttle, then crawl and eventually totter on uncertain legs to return whatever item it was to his sister, only to repeat the process until he, (or more usually, she) got tired of the game.

Mike pondered whether to stay in the office and go to meet Akin from there, but then decided he'd brave the traffic and head home to grab some time with his family and have supper — Ronke's culinary talents represented another reason to love her as much as he did. He summoned his secretary, told her to alert the driver that he was on his way down, packed up his briefcase and headed for the lift.

"Good evening *Baba'beji*, welcome. How was your day?"

"We thank God Ma, and yours?" Mike greeted his mother-in-law in what had become almost a nightly ritual.

"As you can hear, your wife is giving your son a bath. I don't know where that boy got his *obun* mentality from. I have never come across a child so averse to having a wash.

Why he can't be like his *omo-jeje* sister is beyond me. I'll go and tell her you're home."

"He's just missing his Daddy, that's all — after all he's been cooped up with several women all day... enough to drive any man to distraction." He smiled and swayed back to avoid the friendly cuff aimed at him half-heartedly by Ronke's mum. "I'll go and sort him out. Funke *nko*?" he asked, looking around for his daughter.

"Bathed, fed and probably fast asleep by now."

Mike could hear Fola's indignant yells as he approached the bathroom. It was true that his son had never been enthusiastic about having a bath, but Mike was convinced that Fola was much less upset when his father gave him a bath. Ronke's view was that she wasn't surprised since she didn't have any time for 'the silly boys games you guys play in the bath'.

"Hey, chap, what's going on?" The boy stopped protesting

at the sound of his father's voice, and reached up with both arms to be rescued.

"Your father has come back, so you've stopped screaming like someone whose eyes were being gouged out with a hot iron, *abi*?

Ronke tilted her face up for Mike's kiss. "*Oya*, carry your noisy child and let me get some peace." She passed the still whimpering Fola to his father, handing him a towel at the same time. "I've laid his clothes out on the bed. Try not to wake Little Madam up, if this banshee's howling hasn't done so already."

"Yes, dear."

Her brother's howling had indeed woken Funke up. She smiled placidly at her father, ignoring her brother's attempts to reach out to her. She pulled herself up to a sitting position, and oversaw the process of Fola being creamed and dressed with a faintly magisterial air, spoiled only by her sticking her thumb in her mouth as she did so. Once the process was complete, and Fola released, she removed her thumb from her mouth, pointed at Mike and said "Dada." Mike beamed at his daughter as he picked her up, scooped up his son from the floor of the closet where he was investigating his mother's shoes, and went in search of his wife and dinner.

"*Baba'beji*, won't you change out of your work clothes before you eat something?"

"No, Ma, I still have to go to a meeting this evening, I just thought I would come home and see you guys before, because the twins would probably be asleep by the time I get back."

"Meeting? This evening?" Ronke asked as she came into the dining room with the steward in tow bearing Mike's supper on a tray.

"Fraid so, dear. Hopefully it won't be too late."

"Where's this meeting?"

Mike was about to answer when he remembered that Akin had asked him not to say anything to Ronke. He hesitated, and then decided to come clean. "Akin asked me to meet him at one of the minister's guest houses, but wouldn't say what it was about, and asked me to keep it under my hat."

Ronke's brow furrowed. "Hmm. . . probably more of their political shenanigans. Well, you know my views on that subject—and on your friend."

Mike sighed. For some reason, Ronke had never warmed to Akin, and it hadn't got any better over the years. She had gone as far as suggesting that Mike seriously consider getting another job outside government. It was the one thing upon which they did not quite see eye to eye.

He'd tried to avoid the subject since then, but he knew it hadn't really gone away.

"Yes, dear."

Mike decided, given Akin's strictures about discretion, to dismiss his driver, and drive himself to the guest house. He had a rough idea where it was, and managed to find it without difficulty. As he parked, he noted Akin's SUV was nowhere to be seen amongst the few cars parked around the house. As a steward let him in, he was surprised to see Akin sitting in the sitting room, nursing a beer.

"I didn't see your car out there," he said by way of greeting.

"No, you didn't. What are you drinking? *James, wey de suya?*" This last was directed at the steward.

"Sah, they just brought it; I was about to serve it when *Oga* arrived," James stammered in reply.

"*Oya,* bring it quick and bring one Star for *Oga,* then vamoose. I'll call you if I need you again."

Mike wasn't really hungry, but he could never resist good peppery suya, especially when accompanied by ice-cold beer, as this was. He waited for James to leave, then turned to Akin with a raised brow. "So, what's all this James Bond stuff about?"

Akin got up to make sure that James had indeed retreated from the kitchen to the boys' quarters at the rear. He returned, and sat down heavily.

"The minister is going to resign in a couple of weeks or so in order to run for governor of his state. I'm going with him to help run his campaign. Not only does that mean that you're likely to be out of a job, it also means that the minister only has a short time left in which he can directly influence federal appointments. If he doesn't get the president to sign off on those appointments before he leaves, it's likely that the current minister of state will be promoted, and get to make the appointments. Both the minister and I want to avoid that — he'll just pack the place with his kinsmen, whether they're any good or not."

"Interesting. As it happens, Ronke has been leaning on me to look for a job outside government, so — "

"I haven't finished yet," Akin interrupted him with an irritated wave of his hand. "We've worked too hard on the privatisation agenda to have it all undone now by a bunch of cowboys. The only way to make sure that does not happen is to put our people in key positions to make sure they do not fuck it up. Which is where you come in. OP3 needs a new head. You're it."

"Do I get a say in this?" OP3 was the Office for Public and Private Partnership, a federal parastatal that oversaw and executed government's privatisation and commercialization agenda. It was a key cog in the privatisation machine. Mike could think of worse things to do — he would be his own boss, at least on a day to day basis, but— "Doesn't OP3 come under the ministry's supervision? If, as you say, the MoS is promoted, he could frustrate everything OP3 does, or wants to do, couldn't he?" Mike was using the office jargon for the minister of state.

Akin smiled faintly. "I think you sometimes forget that you met me in this system. Do you really think we hadn't thought of that? The statement that announces your appointment will also say that the OP3 will now be supervised by the Office of the President, which neatly takes you out of the ministry."

"How long do I have to decide? I need to talk it over with Ronke first."

"Not long. As I said, we're out of here in a couple of weeks, so the deed will need to be done in the next few days. Your call."

Mike was so preoccupied as he drove home, he unconsciously had started driving towards his old bachelor pad in Jabi before realising he was heading the wrong way. He swore under his breath as he corrected course. OP3 was certainly an attractive option, especially if no longer under the aegis of the ministry. With a relatively free hand, he might have an unparalleled opportunity to help set up several enterprises free from the leaden hand of government control, and set them on the path to productivity, wealth and employment creation — and swell government coffers in the process. On the whole, he thought, it was an opportunity too good to turn down. Now, how to convince Ronke.

As Mike pondered what line of approach would work best with his wife, he would have been bemused had he been aware of a scene unfolding at the ministry guest house he had just left. James the steward re-emerged from the Boys Quarters in response to Akin's telephoned summons. He let Akin out, and waited until he was sure that he had left the premises and hadn't forgotten anything he might want to come back for. Then, before clearing up the remnants of the suya, and the empty beer bottles and glasses, he reached underneath the coffee table in the middle of the room and retrieved the black electronic gadget that the man from the SSS has given him earlier in the day, together with five thousand naira, and a scrap of paper with a telephone number on it that he was to call as soon as Akin and whomever he was meeting with had left. James had a minor panic when he couldn't find the scrap of paper in his pocket, then remembered that he had folded it and put it in his wallet for safe keeping. He went into the kitchen and dialled the number he had been given on his phone.

"Hello, hello?"

"Yes?" It didn't sound like the same person who had given him the number.

"Sah, this is James from the guesthouse. They told me to ring when *Oga* has left."

"Where is the...thing you were given?"

"Sah, I have it."

"Good. I am going to send someone now to collect it. He will give you a piece of paper with this same number on it. Only when he gives you that paper should you give him the package—is that clear?"

"Yes sah." The phone went dead.

Ten minutes later, a nondescript looking young man knocked on the door.

"You have it?" The man proffered a piece of paper that had some numbers on it. James checked that they were the same numbers he had been given earlier, and then passed the gadget to the young man, who briefly checked it then thrust it into one of the folds of the flowing native costume he was wearing. "Give me the paper you were given earlier," he said. James complied.

The man gave him a couple of crisp 500 naira notes. "If you like yourself, keep your mouth shut about this, you hear?" The calm way in which the man spoke to James made the words seem even more menacing.

"Yes sah," he stuttered in reply, but the man had already wheeled round and merged into the shadows.

"Hey babes, still awake?" Mike slipped into the bedroom. Ronke was half sitting up in bed, reading glasses perched on the end of her nose going through some papers. She looked up with a smile.

"Nah, I'm fast asleep and snoring as you can see. How was your meeting?"

"Interesting. The twins asleep?"

"Long time ago. Why aren't you answering me?"

Mike had been undressing as he spoke, and now sat on the bed to take off his socks. "I will dear, but do you think I could have a quick shower first?"

A few minutes later he was lying in bed next to her and telling her about Akin's proposal. Ronke heard him through, and then turned to look at him. "Well?"

"Well what?"

"What are you going to do?"

"I think it would be a great opportunity."

"Maybe, but that's not what I asked you."

"I think I should go for it."

Ronke was quiet for a minute, then moved away from him and sat up straighter.

"You know how I feel about Akin and his political friends . . . this whole thing makes me feel uneasy, I have to tell you. Maybe Akin and the minister leaving is God's way of saying it's time for you to move on."

"Since when did you get all religious on me?" Mike replied, trying to lighten the mood.

Ronke wasn't playing. "Seriously, I think you should think long and hard about this."

"Okay darling. Let's sleep on it. We don't have to decide anything tonight, do we?"

"No, we don't." She turned and smiled at him with a glint in her eye. "When was the last time you made love to your wife, Sir?"

"Thought you'd never ask."

CHAPTER 4

Abuja, Nigeria

AS MIKE DRIED HIMSELF IN THE CHANGING ROOMS after his post-exercise class shower, he swore he would never again allow himself to get as out of shape as he had over the last year. He had seriously underestimated the amount of travel and interagency politicking involved in the OP3 job, not to talk of the added complexity of reporting to the presidency. It all seemed a long time ago that he had entered the Presidential Villa for the first time to meet the president's chief of staff ahead of being sworn in by Mr President. He had slowly learned the ropes of the various protocol procedures attached to the presidency, and the way in which his new role opened doors in a way that he had not imagined. Unfortunately, neither had he imagined the obligations that came with the role—he doubted that there was a state in the country he had not visited in the course of the last year, attending some wedding, funeral or thanksgiving service as a guest of some minister, senator or governor. Ronke had not really said much, but he knew she was not pleased by the amount of time he spent away from home, especially since she hadn't been that keen on him taking the job in the first place. He had promised her that they would all go away together as a family for three weeks at least to the UK and the States this summer, and he made a mental note to get his PA to make the provisional travel bookings for Ronke's approval. Still, there were some perks to the job—a shiny red diplomatic passport, a much larger and competent staff, and some real job satisfaction. He had also made some useful contacts in the security agencies in the presidency, and indeed, it was with one of the brighter young operatives that he had come to the exercise class.

"Sir, for an old man, you're not that bad", Adamu said with a smile, as he got dressed on the bench next to Mike.

"It is your father that is an old man, you this foolish boy. You wait, in a few weeks I'll be kicking your butt," Mike responded in kind. "This is quite a nice club. How does one join?"

"Not a problem Sir. A friend of mine owns it. I'll see if he's around today and we can get the ball rolling with forms and the like."

Mike wondered, not for the first time, why Adamu, who was clearly a very bright, well-educated and well-spoken young man had ended up doing what he did. He made a note to ask him to dinner at home and get to know him a bit better.

They finished changing and wandered to the bar that overlooked the tennis courts, and in the distance, parts of the golf course. A few middle-aged men were pretending to play tennis, while others sat watching them drinking beer — by the looks of the beer bellies on display, both on the court and off it, playing tennis was a distant second to beer drinking as a pastime for this lot. A pretty young waitress showed Mike and Adamu to a table in a corner.

"What can I get you, Sir?"

"Can I have a chicken Caesar salad and a small bottle of still water with ice?" Adamu asked.

"Of course, Sir. . . and for you Sir?" she said, this last to Mike.

"Make that two."

"Right away Sir. Would you like some nuts to nibble on in the meantime?"

"Sure."

As the waitress turned to walk away, Adamu asked, "Is Chike in today?"

"I will find out for you Sir. Whom shall I say is asking?"

"Just tell him Adamu."

"Yes Sir," she said and walked away.

Mike found himself admiring the waitress' cute behind as she walked away. "Are all the staff here as well-trained and well spoken as she is?" he asked Adamu.

"Well Sir, unless I'm much mistaken, my friend Chike who owns this place is heading this way, so you can hear it straight from the horse's mouth," Adamu replied with a laugh.

A stocky young man wearing shorts and a polo shirt was walking towards them, stopping to greet several patrons along the way. As he got to their table, Adamu stood up and hugged him as they exchanged greetings. "Chike, meet my *oga*, Mr Mike Anako, the head of OP3. Chike and I were classmates in secondary school, and he owns this place," Adamu said.

"You're very welcome Sir," Chike said, bowing slightly as he shook Mike's hand.

"This is a great place you have here, I'm very impressed with the facilities and with your staff."

"Thanks Sir, we try our best." Chike beamed broadly.

"*Oga* was asking me about joining. Can you sort out forms and stuff?"

"Right away. He turned and waved at one of his staff. "Please get me a prospective membership pack from the office," he said to the man when he arrived. The man vanished and returned in quick time with a very impressively put together brochure that Mike started leafing through. It really was an impressive establishment, with a wide range of facilities. He winced slightly when he saw what the joining fee and annual subscriptions were, but, he reasoned, this sort of quality didn't come cheap.

The salads arrived, and were actually very good. Mike thought to himself that he could get used to this place.

Lagos, Nigeria

Mike woke up with a start. He did not recall falling asleep after leaving Ijebu-Ode, but perhaps it was inevitable given the generous helpings of pounded yam and vegetable soup with goat meat that his mother-in-law had plied him with, despite his (admittedly feeble) protests. She took one look at his slightly trimmer figure, the results of quite a few exercise classes at the gym in Abuja and some dietary restraint on his part, and informed him that no son-in-law of hers was going to be allowed to waste away to nothingness in front of her, irrespective of what anyone else, her daughter included, thought. She was too good a cook, and he too faithful a disciple of her art to resist for long. He consoled himself that he would skip supper tonight and get a hard session in at the gym in his hotel before the meeting tomorrow with some potential investors in the planned privatisation of the remaining government holdings in the Lagos port. He was trying to work out where exactly they'd got to when his phone rang.

"Distinguished chief of staff, to what do mere mortals like us owe a call from your excellency?"

Akin's reply was unprintable. He at least appeared to have restored some of his sense of humour after the stress and tension of the election for state governor he and the former minister had just been through. Even by Nigerian standards, it had been a pretty turbulent process, involving several physical bust-ups and court cases right from the party primaries through to, and after the main election itself, which had finally ended in victory for the former minister, now governor-elect, and shortly to be his excellency the governor. There had been much speculation in the media as to the make up of Big Man's (as the former minister was now apparently known) new government, and

Akin's name had featured prominently as being appointed the governor's chief of staff.

"Are you back in Lagos?"

"Just approaching now, from Ijebu-Ode via Epe. I stopped to see my in-laws. You know Prof hasn't been well recently, although you'd never have thought it given the amount of brandy he and his cronies put away last night."

"Good boy. At least you have sensible people for in-laws, unlike those Gboko beasts that make up Sade's family."

"You let her catch you referring to her people like that. Besides, why Gboko? I thought she was from Ekiti?"

"Never mind that. Where are you staying?"

"The Wheatsheaf . . . where else?"

"I gather you're meeting some people tomorrow about this Ports thing. *Oga* has an interest, and wants to send someone to have a chat with you before the meeting tomorrow. Is it okay if she comes to see you at the hotel later, say about 9ish?"

"This isn't one of your political scratch my back I scratch your back jobs, is it?"

"You mean the same ones that got you your job?"

"Touché. What's this person's name?"

"Not sure. Will check and text it to you."

Mrs. Tayo Adebisi was one of those vaguely decadent Lagos women in her late 40s or early 50s that were a near-permanent fixture in glossy style magazines. Overweight, with artificially bleached skin and execrable dress sense, Mike disliked her on sight. Her vaguely flirtatious manner didn't help either. Mike tried to not let his feelings show as he sat across a low coffee table from her in one of the hotel's excellently appointed lounges.

"His excellency said I should come and see you for your help on the Ports matter," she said, looking at him somewhat coquettishly. "We are working together on this business, and he said you can be able to help us."

Mike winced internally at this wanton mauling of the English language. "So, that's why I come see you sah," she continued. She leaned forward, revealing even more of her ample cleavage, and dropped her voice. "I think Mr Akin has briefed you on the matter, *abi*?"

"He did no such thing, neither did anyone else. What, exactly, is the help you need from me?"

She sat back and wrinkled her nose as if perceiving a particularly nasty smell. "Ah, ah, sah, you want me to use my whole mouth to talk?"

Mike felt himself starting to move from impatience to annoyance. "Frankly, I really don't care whether you use half, a quarter or your whole mouth to talk. I have an early start tomorrow, so I would appreciate an early night — can you help me by saying what exactly it is you want from me?" He suspected he knew what the answer was, but wanted to force her to say it.

She looked around the lounge, and then said, "Let's talk somewhere privately now. *Oga* Akin said you were staying here?"

Mike eyed her balefully. "Where I may or may not be staying is my business. For the last time, are you going to tell me what it is you want from me? Because, if not, I am going to have to leave."

She looked at him as one would regard an idiot child. "I don't know why excellency sent me to you if this is how you want to be doing o," she muttered half to herself. She hesitated, as though weighing something up, then evidently decided to take the plunge. She heaved a sigh, then leant forward again. "Excellency is working with us on our bid to take over the Ports, and we need your help. Of course, we will look after you."

"By all means feel free to put in a bid, which will be considered with all the other bids in the same open and transparent manner." He thought of asking her about her comment about "looking after" him, but decided he didn't want to go there.

She rolled her eyes, and hissed. Without saying anything more she heaved herself out of the chair and headed to the door, pulling out her phone as she went. Mike had no doubt that she would be straight on the phone to Akin, or his excellency to complain about his attitude. He decided he didn't have the energy tonight to engage in a discussion with anyone about the matter, but knew it was inevitable that, sooner rather than later, he'd have either Akin, or even his excellency on the phone complaining. He headed to the lifts, switching of both his phones as he went.

Mike realised that as his alarm went off that he hadn't called Ronke and the children the previous night. He sat up somewhat groggily in bed and groped for his phone on the bedside table. He eventually located it, turned off the alarm and turned on the lamp by the bed, swinging his feet on to the floor and turning on the phone as he did so. He left it on the bed and walked across to the bathroom. As he stood at the toilet relieving himself, he could hear the phone pinging away as emails and text messages flooded in.

Ignoring the phone, he located his gym kit and got changed, and only then did he check the phone. As he suspected, Ronke had sent him a couple of texts, as had Akin. Mike grimaced to himself, knowing what was coming. He decided he could ignore Akin until he'd done his workout, but his wife was another proposition entirely. He called her number several times, cursing the mobile phone networks as he did so, until the phone eventually started to ring. He was on the verge of putting it down when he heard Ronke's somewhat sleepy voice. "What sort of time do you call this?"

"The best time to speak to one's lady wife. How are you babes? Sorry I didn't call last night." He went on to explain what had happened with the bleached woman Akin had sent to him the previous night, and why he'd turned off his phones. "As I thought, there have been several hundred texts this morning, all of which are doubtlessly asking what I think I'm playing at."

"Well, what are you playing at?" Ronke asked in her usual direct style. "You know what my views are — time to get out of that blasted job and get back to the real world. There's a limit to how long you can play with these people before you get smeared with their shit."

"I am getting tired of the whole thing. Perhaps I'll tell the Villa when we get back from our trip that I want out. Talking of which, did the office send you the provisional bookings?"

"Yes, they did. Don't change the subject. When are you getting out?"

"When we get back dear. I promise" He was surprised how easily it slipped out.

"Fine. I'll hold you to it."

Mike was surprised how hard he was able to push himself on the exercise bike in the gym. It was true after all that practice made perfect — he was now able to sustain cycling for an entire hour at speeds in excess of 30 m.p.h. Or perhaps it was because he had been turning over last night's events in his head. It was quite clear to him that his excellency and Akin were running some kind of racket with the bleached whale they'd sent to see him last night, and that he was key to ensuring the success of the deal in his OP3 role; of that he had little doubt. He'd promised Ronke he would get out when they got back from their trip — perhaps he ought to hand his resignation in before the trip? On second thought, that might not be wise — they could simply stitch it up while he was away, and he would return to a *fait accompli*. Perhaps he ought to just play along for now? After all, what was the worst that could happen — they got him sacked? Well, he was going anyway, so they could get stuffed.

He didn't know then how much he would come to rue that decision.

Later that evening, Mike and Akin were sitting in a bar overlooking the lagoon, sipping cold beers. Mike realised he would have to have this out with Akin sooner or later.

"My friend, you're getting in way above your head on this one," Akin said, carefully setting his glass down.

"In what way? It's pretty simple — there are at least four bids from companies who have long and deep knowledge of managing port services, and are bidding to do it significantly cheaper than your friend. There's probably not much between the four bids I'm talking about, but the gulf between them and your friend's is huge."

Akin waved an impatient hand. "Maybe, but as I think Mrs Adebisi told you, Excellency has an interest in this matter."

"So? Does that mean I should sanction something I know to be crap? Wasn't it exactly this sort of shit I was appointed to put an end to?"

Akin had the grace to look vaguely uncomfortable. "Look, there are wheels within wheels. To be frank with you, I am not sure that even I know the whole story here, but I know enough to know that this won't end well if you carry on with this your stubborn goat approach."

"Akin, are you threatening me?"

"No, you fool. I'm trying to protect you."

Igore, Nigeria

His excellency 'Big Man' was in a foul mood. His recent victory at the polls was not turning out to be quite as he had expected. His defeated opponent was threatening to take the matter to an election tribunal, alleging widespread 'irregularities' (all of which the hypocritical bastard had helped to plan before defecting to the opposition after failing to wrest the party's nomination from Big Man) and every half-wit in the party was now besieging his house, seeking one appointment or the other (and consuming prodigious amounts of food and booze in the process). The glorified motor park tout sitting before him now, loudly chewing on a piece of goat meat and slurping straight from a large bottle of Guinness was a case in point. Rejoicing under the somewhat improbable name of Casablanca, he had been at the head of a band of several thugs who had provided 'security' at Big Man's election rallies, and had disrupted those of the opposition. This, he reminded Big Man in between loud belches, that he had been key to his victory, and 'the boys' now needed looking after by himself, Casablanca. So he would need an suitable appointment to the state cabinet, such as commissioner for Youth, Sports and Culture. Big Man almost laughed out loud. Politics did make for strange bedfellows, it was true, but the line had to be drawn somewhere. Casablanca in the cabinet? Hell, no. He was wondering how to fob him off when his phone rang. It was Chief. Oh, great.

"Hello, Chief?"

"My brother, how now? It seems we have a problem?"

"Hold on, let me just find somewhere quiet". He stood up, with an apologetic wave to his guest and he retreated to an inner sanctum. "What's the problem?"

"It seems that foolish *oyinbo* boy at OP3 is refusing to cooperate. Tayo went to see him yesterday about the Ports thing, and he was insulting her and speaking grammar. You know what our deal was, so tidy up before *water begin to pass gari o*."

"Don't worry, Chief, I'll take care of it." He returned to the outer room, where Casablanca had now demolished both the meat and the bottle of Guinness. "Another Guinness?" he asked. He raised his voice and bellowed in the general direction of the kitchen. "Another Guinness for my friend — do you people want to starve the hon commissioner to death?"

Casablanca stretched his rubbery lips in a horrible grin. "For the Big Man *ke*!"

Big Man acknowledged the greeting with the thumbs up election sign. "I have one small job for you."

Abuja, Nigeria

Mike was dog-tired. The meetings with the potential investors in the Ports project had been more demanding than he had anticipated. Each of the consortia had insisted on their day in court, with glossy presentations of varying levels of complexity and persuasiveness. The other members of the assessment panel were of course unaware of the background noise involving Akin, Mrs Adebisi and Big Man, but the initial soundings suggested that that particular bid has been the least persuasive. Nonetheless, they now had to whittle down the bids to three, with a recommendation to government as to whom should be given preferred bidder status once the Central Bank and Ministry of Finance had completed their due diligence checks. He sat back even lower in the backseat of the SUV, as he was driven home from the airport. He could at least shelve the whole thing from his mind until he got back from holiday.

He did not notice the nondescript people carrier that had been following the SUV from the airport. Casablanca sat in front beside the driver, whom he had personally selected from among his boys because of his knowledge of Abuja's roads. Another two thugs, Razor and Morocco, were in the middle seats, peering over the shoulders of the pair in front.

"Make sure you don't lose them o. And I don't want to hear any foolish story about you getting lost. There is a lot hanging on this job, so don't fuck it up, or you people and I will wear the same trouser."

"*Oga* Casablanca, when have we ever disappointed you?" Razor said in his peculiar sing-song voice.

"Na you sabi. Just don't fumble."

Suleija, Nigeria

Razor and Morocco lounged on the bed in one of the rooms at the hotel that they were staying in while on the job. The air hung thick with the smoke from the joints they and their two female companions were smoking. The ceiling fan struggled to move either the hot and dank air, or the mosquitoes. None of the room's occupants were particularly bothered—after all, their bellies were full, and they were both drunk and stoned, courtesy of the one hundred thousand-naira advance that Casablanca had provided. This time tomorrow, the job would be done, and they'd both be back in Igore, with the balance of another hundred thousand that they'd been promised. Meanwhile, the beer and *ogogoro* were flowing, there were women on tap, and it was on someone else's bill. What was not to like?

CHAPTER 5

Abuja, Nigeria

MIKE WOKE WITH A START. HE'D BEEN HAVING A weird dream that involved his late parents playing with his twins. That he had been dreaming at all was unusual enough in itself, but this one seemed particularly unusual.

A few hours later, he was trying his best to herd his family together for the trip to the airport. As usual, Ronke was making last minute changes to the packing list for the twins, whose suitcase had been reopened for the umpteenth time. Both toddlers seemed to regard this as a game put on especially for their entertainment, which only served to increase their mother's irritability–Mike eventually had to remove both twins from under their mother's feet, which meant that he then had to cope with them wanting to grab passports and boarding passes. Eventually, they were temporarily imprisoned in their high chairs, which in turn led to loud howls of protest. To make matters worse, one of the drivers had failed to turn up, so Mike would now have to drive one of the cars to the airport himself. Not for the first time, he wondered why they needed quite so many suitcases— they were only going to be away for a month, and they would doubtless be doing more shopping while away, so the return journey would be even more hellish.

Eventually, all was ready, or so it seemed. One of the SUVs refused to start—the idiot driver had left the headlights on when washing the cars earlier, and now the battery was flat.

"Look, you guys go ahead with the driver. I'll catch up with you once I get this one started," Mike said to Ronke.

"Are you sure? Won't you be late?"

"I'll be fine. The protocol chaps will meet you there and sort you out—besides, we're already checked in so it's just dropping off the bags."

"Okay babes, see you shortly," She leaned forward and kissed him, and got into the SUV.

Mike watched them drive off, and then turned to the steward. "Have you called the mechanic?"

"Yessah, he say he is on the way"

Suleija, Nigeria

Morocco woke up with a start and looked at the clock on his phone. "*Shege!*" he swore out loud, and pushed the sleeping naked girl away from him. He hastily pulled on his clothes and went next door, banging on Razor's room door. "*Ol' boy, time don go o!*" he shouted. Razor's cannabis and whisky-befuddled mind, never sharp at the best of times, seemed particularly leaden this morning. What was wrong with that foolish boy, banging his door and shouting at the top of his voice? Then suddenly he remembered. Springing up, he was halfway to the door when he realised he was not wearing any clothes. He fumbled around for his clothes, ignoring the equally naked girl. Morocco continued to bang on the door. "*I don ready, I dey come – go start the moto.*"

They raced down the road towards Abuja. Neither of them wanted to think about Casablanca's wrath if they screwed this job up. They both knew that they had overdone the booze and cannabis last night, which would only make matters worse for them. Anything, almost even being caught, was better than screwing up. They were two really desperate men now.

Abuja, Nigeria

The mechanic eventually arrived with a new battery and a set of jump leads. Mike decided he didn't have the time to wait for the battery to be changed, so he got the mechanic to jump-start the SUV using the jump leads from his car's battery. The Toyota's engine initially spluttered, then roared into life. Once he was satisfied that it wouldn't conk out again, he got behind the wheel and headed for the airport.

Driving like lunatics, Razor and Morocco swerved in and out of traffic, occasionally driving on the wrong side of the road, such was their desperation. As Morocco careened through the traffic, Razor struggled to load the weapons, frequently losing a few rounds as the car lurched from side to side. Eventually he gave up, snapping magazines into both rifles. What they had would have to do...

Lagos, Nigeria

Chief got up from the breakfast table. His doctor had managed to get him to modify his dietary habits—gone were the thick slices of white bread and mountains of oily eggs and sausages, and in came pap sweetened with sweeteners—on the whole, he much preferred the former, but hey... He stretched and yawned. He wondered a little impatiently how the governor-elect was getting on with resolving the Ports issue; it was about time the problem went away, one way or the other. That was the problem with politicians: all mouth and no action. Well, if he wouldn't deal with it, then Chief would have to.

Igore, Nigeria

"Big Man, this is Casablanca. We have sorted out that job, but. . . ." Unusually, Casablanca sounded not quite as cocksure as he usually did.

"Any problem?" Big Man replied sharply.

"Well, not really. The foolish boys I sent got a little carried away."

"Meaning?"

Casablanca hesitated. *"Ebe like say the people don die o."*

"Are you mad? Which people?"

"Excellency, not on the phone. I will brief you when I get back." The phone went dead.

Bida, Nigeria

It was one of those beer parlours that seemed to spring up in and around motor parks across the country. A variety of alcoholic and soft drinks were available, along with cigarettes, kola nuts and assorted sweets and snacks. Police sometimes set up road blocks near these places, the better to extort from both passing traffic and the beer parlours. Indeed, Razor and Morocco had been relieved of 200 naira by the policemen, which they handed over with forced grins and banter. The pair were certainly not bantering and grinning now. Each sat staring into space, occasionally taking a pull from their joints, or sipping from the glasses of *ogogoro* in front of the rapidly emptying bottle. If they'd been in any doubt about the scale on which they'd screwed up, they had been swiftly disabused of that idea by Casablanca's fury when they reported to him. He had swiftly seen through the limp excuses they had tried to offer about the car having mechanical problems; he knew as well as they did that they could simply, as they had so often done in the past, relieved a passing motorist of his or her car instead. He had come uncomfortably close to guessing the root of the problem when he suggested, quite forcefully, that it was his own fault for giving them too much money for operating expenses; that he would expect a very detailed reckoning upon their return was not something the marauding pair were in any doubt about. In the meantime, their instructions were to lay low and avoid Igore or any contact with Casablanca for the next two weeks at least.

Abuja, Nigeria

He'd frequently driven past the National Hospital, but had never actually been inside it. Even as he sat, numb with shock, in what passed for the Casualty Department, staring at his blood stained hands and clothing, he couldn't quite bring himself to believe why he was here. He vaguely remembered swearing as he hit a patch of traffic as he approached the airport. Self-important government functionaries in their convoys with flashing lights and blaring sirens were bad enough at the best of times, but not today, please, he had a plane to catch. The first sign that all was not well was seeing the cars ahead of him pulling frantic U-turns or even reversing at speed. People waiting at bus stops joined the stampede, shouting about armed robbers 'operating' further up the road. Oh shit, he thought. He was contemplating turning round and trying to find an alternative route when he saw that the traffic in the distance was starting to move again. He heaved a sigh of relief, and moved off past the cars that had started to change course, and were now trying to revert to the original direction of travel. Unsurprisingly, there had been a few collisions in the chaos, which he managed to navigate his way past. He approached the point where the original incident had happened . . . and the nightmare began.

"Sir?" The voice broke into Mike's reverie. He looked up to see a youngish looking man dressed in theatre clothes. "Mr Anako?"

"Yes."

"Sir, my name is Dr Adenuga, one of the surgical registrars. Please come with me, the consultant would like to talk to you."

"Are they okay?" Mike demanded.

"Sir, I think it's better you come and speak with Mr Ajayi, he's just getting changed."

Mike's heart sank. He nodded, and followed the young doctor up two flights of stairs. He was led through a pair of double doors underneath a sign saying "Theatres 1 & 2", and was shown into a small room on the left. "I'll go and tell Mr Ajayi you're here."

It seemed like hours, but was probably only a few minutes when the door opened again, and another, slightly older, man entered, also dressed in theatre greens.

"Mr Anako?" Mike nodded. "My name is Femi Ajayi, and I'm the surgical consultant on call. We've been in theatre with the casualties from the incident on the airport road earlier. I'm afraid the news isn't good—we weren't able to save any of them . . . I'm so sorry."

Mike felt as if he'd been kicked in the stomach. In truth, the small part of him that was still capable of rational thought was not surprised—the carnage he'd seen at the scene was beyond description—but it still felt like a hammer blow to hear the doctor say those words. He realised the doctor was still talking " . . . my deepest condolences. Unfortunately, because of the nature of the circumstances of death, we will have to refer the case to the coroner."

"What do you mean? Does the coroner get involved in road traffic accidents?"

Mr Ajayi stared at him for a minute. "Mr Anako, three of the four victims, including some of your family, appear to have been the victims of gunshot wounds; the post-mortem will be able to clarify that."

CHAPTER 6

Victoria Garden City Lagos, three months later

MIKE SAT STARING AT THE TV WITHOUT REALLY seeing it. He could hear his sister bustling around in the kitchen, getting supper ready. She had really been a pillar of strength throughout the horrendous last few weeks. It was Elizabeth who had overseen the funeral arrangements, liaising with Ronke's parents and with the church. She had insisted that he come and stay with her, and pointed out that her home in Lagos was a lot closer to Ronke's parents in Ijebu-Ode, than was his flat in Abuja; she didn't have to remind him that it was also closer to his family's final resting place in the Adesanya family plot in the church cemetery.

Elizabeth had striven valiantly to try and keep his spirits up and to console him; he really could not have asked for more. Femi, his brother-in-law, had also been a strong, if slightly more silent, support. Mike was truly grateful for the support, but he knew he now had to start the process of getting back on his own two feet.

Elizabeth came into the room with a tray, which she set in front of him. The heady aroma of fried plantain accompanied her. She removed the covers from the dishes. "*Oya*, I've fried you some of the rotten plantain you like to eat." She sat down across the coffee table directly opposite him. "What do you want to drink?"

"Elizabeth thanks so much. Cold water is fine." She called the steward to bring the water.

Mike knew his sister was going to sit in front of him until he made at least a token effort to eat his supper. He dutifully helped himself to a small portion of plantain and stew, and began to eat.

"I've been thinking that I need to get back on my feet . . . I can't stay here forever, and I do need to start to get on with my life. I'm planning on going back to Abuja next week."

"To do what? I thought you'd resigned?"

"Not quite. I've been on compassionate leave for six weeks. I need to go and tidy things up, prepare handover notes and so on. And I need to sort out the flat." He winced involuntarily as he thought about going back to the memories of Ronke, Fola and Funke.

Elizabeth eyed him with some concern. "I've heard you. Finish your food and we can talk about it when Femi gets back."

Mike knew this was her attempt to kick the subject into the tall grass. He smiled to take the sting out of his words. "No, we won't. I'm really going back. I will go and see Prof and Mama in Ijebu tomorrow, and will probably stay for a couple of days before coming back and heading off to Abuja."

"As you wish."

Ijebu-Ode, Nigeria

The drive from Lagos to Ijebu-Ode seemed to take a lot longer than it usually did, even allowing for the volume of traffic and the state of the roads; or perhaps he had just been lost in his thoughts about his family, as he so often seemed to be these days.

As the car crawled through the traffic jam created by road construction in Ijebu-Ode, Mike's attention was caught by the headlines in one of the newspapers being held up by one of the several roadside vendors. "Controversy Surrounds Port Privatisation Project". Mike wound down the window and called the vendor over, rummaging in the cup holder for the one and two hundred naira notes he habitually kept there for just this purpose. He bought a couple of papers and wound the window up again, shutting out the hordes of hustlers seizing the opportunity to push their assorted wares. He cast his eye over the story. As usual, it was littered with poor grammar and spelling, but the broad story was that several of the bidders were preemptively raising the alarm about rumour that a decision had been made in principle to award the concession to Adolak Holdings, the company that Akin had indicated Big Man was involved with. According to the story, the OP3 panel that sat in his absence had included Adolak in the shortlist of three preferred bidders that had been approved by the relevant minister and was to be considered for final ratification at the upcoming meeting of the Federal Executive Council. Mike pursed his lips, as he wondered which of his colleagues had been compromised... not that he cared any longer. He scanned the rest of the paper, casting it aside as he realised they had arrived at his in-law's home. After a short delay, the gates were opened by one of the security men, and they drove in. Mike got down a little stiffly, and walked up the short set of steps to the broad veranda that ran along the entire front of the bungalow. Ronke's Mum's passion for horticulture was evident in the forest of potted, hanging and climbing plants that festooned the veranda with an explosion of colour and scents. He entered the living room and looked round. The housemaid who had let him in said in response to his unspoken question that "*Oga* is in the study. Mummy went to the doctor but she will be back soon."

Mike nodded an acknowledgment and turned to head toward his father-in-law's study, which was at the end of a corridor leading off the left side of the living room. As he approached, he could hear the strains of the classical music that Ronke's Dad was so fond of. He tapped on the door and entered. Mike was struck, not for the first time, with the thought that his father-in-law was the archetype of the absent-minded professor from central casting. He was leaning back in an overstuffed, cracked leather chair, his feet propped up on a stool, peering through half-moon glasses on a string at a large volume on his lap. He had a highlighter pen in his hand, which he occasionally applied to the tome open in front of him.

Mike cleared his throat, prompting prof to look up. It seemed to take him a while to focus. "Oh, hello," he eventually said, "When did you arrive? I didn't hear you come in."

"Good afternoon, Prof, how are you? I just came in from Lagos now. Comfort said Mummy had gone to the doctors . . . hope she's okay?"

"I think so. Maybe she went to get a new prescription for her blood pressure. It's been apparently unstable over the last few weeks. Hardly surprising."

"Indeed." They were both quiet for a while, lost in their thoughts about their shared tragedy. Prof shook his head as if to purge it of the distressing thoughts. "Shift some of those papers and find somewhere to sit. How about a brandy before Her Majesty your mother gets back and gives us a hard time?"

From the minute that Prof and his wife had given their assent to the proposed union, they had both declared him to be the son they'd never had.

Mike did as he was told, and found somewhere to perch amidst the mass of books, magazines and papers. Ronke's father might have been retired from being one of the country's leading Professors of English, but that did not mean he'd stopped working; he'd written and published no less than half a dozen books since his supposed retirement and move back from Lagos to his home town to live.

Prof produced a bottle from one of the drawers in his desk, and rang the bell for Comfort to fetch a couple of brandy glasses. Once delivered and passed his critical scrutiny of their cleanliness, he poured out generous amounts into the glasses. As Mike had been taught, he did not immediately drink; he slowly swirled the amber liquid around in the glass, then breathed in the aroma deeply, before raising the glass to his lips. He swirled it around in his mouth for a while before swallowing.

"Armagnac, not Cognac. Normandy?"

Prof nodded approvingly. "Not bad for a *kobokobo* boy."

They sat in silence, savouring the drink. Eventually Prof broke the silence.

"You know that part of us died when Ronke and the twins died, don't you? Our only child and only grandchildren, taken away from us so cruelly. . . ." His voice tailed off. "There are days when one wonders what the point is of carrying on, but do you want to know what sustains one?" He paused and turned to look Mike straight in the eye. "I'll tell you. It's the thought of finding the bastards who did this, and then fixing them." There was a hard, rasping quality to Prof's voice that Mike had never heard before.

He swung his feet off the stool and leaned forward towards Mike. "Promise me that you will not rest until you find and exact vengeance from the people who did this to my daughter and grand-children."

Mike was taken aback. This was not the amiable, somewhat eccentric father-in-law he had come to know, respect and even love. "Sir, I don't know about—"

Prof cut him off: "I said, promise me!" He was staring at Mike now.

"I promise."

"Good." Prof leaned back like a man who had just had a huge burden lifted from his shoulders. The amiable eccentric Professor returned. "So, let's see how far we've managed to civilize you. Who composed this piece, and what's it called?" he said, turning up the volume on the stereo.

Abuja, Nigeria, one week later

Mike knew that his days in Abuja were numbered, unless he was never going to fly in and out of the airport again, or until an alternative route was constructed to enable him to avoid the spot where it all happened. Not that you'd know that anything had happened here, he thought, as they drove past—the usual Abuja traffic snarl-up, the crowds at the bus stops, the unregulated taxi cabs and *okadas*— were all still here. He felt a sudden lump in his throat and turned his face away, blinking back the tears.

It wasn't much better in the flat in Maitama. He wandered listlessly from room to room, reminded at each turn of happier times, until the recurrent image of the dark brown coffin and the two smaller white ones intruded again. All of a sudden, the dam burst, and he wept, and wept, and wept in great uncontrollable torrents.

He did not leave the flat for two days. He had barely eaten or drunk anything, despite the entreaties of his steward. He hadn't even been able to sleep properly, tossing and turning, and then waking up in a cold sweat the few times he did manage to fall asleep. He got out of bed and drew back the curtains, staring listlessly out of the window and running his fingers over the stubbly growth on his chin as he watched people, mainly expatriates, playing in the swimming pool below with their children. He felt the knot in his stomach start to tighten again and turned away. He really needed to stop feeling sorry for himself, and start sorting his life out. Suddenly feeling hungry, he called for his steward, and ordered breakfast. He brushed his teeth and threw some cold water on his face, then sat down and devoured stewed eggs and soft, slightly sweet, white bread. Yes, maybe not the healthiest breakfast he had ever had, but what the hell? He was surprised by how much better he felt after breakfast, and, despite two cups of coffee, soon started feeling drowsy.

He slept like a log for several hours, and woke up feeling slightly more human than he had felt in a long time; so human, in fact that he decided that he could do with some exercise, so had headed to the gym. An hour on the cross trainer and a short weights session later, he wondered if he'd overdone it, but it had been useful thinking time. He reviewed what he knew about how Ronke, the children and the driver had met their deaths—all had succumbed to a combination of gunshot wounds and blunt trauma from the subsequent accident, which had been presumed to an armed robbery gone wrong, despite the fact that nothing seemed to have been taken from the victims, other than the property which had gone missing at the hospital and had never been recovered (so much for the caring professionals, Mike thought bitterly). As he stood under the refreshingly cold and powerful shower, Mike realised that the place to start would be with the investigating police, but how to go about that? He didn't know anyone in that world, and although he could ask a few of his contacts, he instinctively felt that he did not want to advertise the fact that he was making enquiries. So, how was he to proceed discreetly?

The answer had come to him when he was making his way out of the club and was approached by the young man who owned and ran the place. He searched his mind for his name while accepting his condolences, and then it came to him.

"Thank you so much Chike, much appreciated" he replied. "How are things with you?"

"We thank God, Sir. Despite all the *wahala* of trying to run a business in this country, we are not doing too badly."

"Keep it up, this town really needs somewhere that sets and keeps proper standards."

"Thank you Sir, we will keep doing our best."

Mike turned to leave, then almost as a casual afterthought, asked "How is your friend Adamu?"

"Oh, he's fine Sir. He was here yesterday and I kicked his ass on the squash court!" Chike replied with a grin.

"Okay-o, greet him for me when you next see him. Or better still, do you have his number?"

"Sure." Chike fumbled in his pocket for his phone, fiddled with it for a moment then started to read out some numbers.

"Hold on," Mike said. He walked over to reception and got a piece of paper and pencil to scribble down the number.

"Many thanks," Mike said to both Chike and the receptionist. He walked back to his car and slung his gym bag in the rear seat. Entering the car, he started the engine and turned the air-conditioning on full blast. Pulling out his phone, he sent a text to Adamu to say he was back in Abuja and asking him to call back. Having done so, he headed for home.

Adamu's call came shortly after Mike had finished his supper.

"Good evening, Sir, this is Adamu."

"Adamu, how now? Thanks for getting back to me so promptly."

"Haba, *oga*, you know I'm your boy anytime. I was so sorry to hear of your bereavement. May the Almighty grant them eternal rest, and grant you the strength to cope with the loss."

"Thank so much. I really appreciate your thoughts and prayers." Mike paused. "I need to pick your brains about something. When would be a good time to meet? I would rather do this face to face and not on the phone."

"No problem *oga*. I got home not that long ago and am just about to have supper but I can meet you after that. Or, if you haven't had supper yet, perhaps you could come join me for supper at my place?"

"Thanks my brother. I just finished eating too. There is no mad rush and I don't want to drag you out again, so we can leave it till tomorrow."

"*Oga*, it will be better if we do it today, because I am travelling abroad with Mr President tomorrow."

"Oh, okay. How long are you away for?"

"Ah, *oga*, that I can't say o," Adamu sounded almost coy.

"No *wahala*. I will come to your place . . ." Mike checked his watch, "say about 9 o'clock? Where do you stay?"

"In Asokoro, just off Yakubu Gowon Way. I will text you the address and let the gate people know you're coming."

A couple of hours later, as Mike drove towards Asokoro, he realised that he didn't REALLY know exactly what Adamu did, beyond knowing that he worked in security. He wasn't the typical gorilla with bulging biceps and semi-solid bone between the ears, and it was Adamu's capacity to think for himself that had first drawn him to Mike's attention. Mike remembered one occasion when several people had been gathered around one of the several flat screen TVs that were a fixture in the offices in the Villa gawping at some Breaking News story on CNN — there had been the usual ill-informed and ignorant speculation which Mike had listened to in amusement and amazement (but knew better than to try and correct), and how he had been surprised by Adamu's well-informed and throughly intelligent comments — delivered in flawless English. Still, he was the only person Mike felt he could approach for assistance now.

Adamu's address was in a fairly new serviced apartment complex. He identified himself to security at the gate and was directed to where he could park, and to which of the three blocks he needed to go. He had to identify himself again in the foyer of Adamu's block, and after a brief conversation on the telephone, one of the desk staff accompanied Mike to the fourth floor and led him to one of the apartments. He tapped gently on the door, which was opened by Adamu himself, dressed in a loose *jalabiyah*. Adamu nodded briefly to Mike's escort, and then invited Mike in with a smile.

"Welcome to my humble abode, Sir"

"Nice place, almost as hard to get into as the Villa," Mike replied with a smile.

Adamu led the way into the sitting room and ushered Mike to one end of a sofa, sitting down at the other end. He pressed a buzzer, and a steward appeared. "What can we offer you?" Adamu asked. "Tea, coffee, soft drinks, beer . . . or would you prefer something a bit stronger?"

Mike looked at the glass on the table in front of Adamu.

"What are you having?"

"It's Jack Daniels, but there's brandy, rum and other stuff if you'd prefer that."

"Maybe a brandy." Mike looked around as Adamu did the honours. He was struck by a school photo on one of the walls that looked like the archetypal English boarding school photo. He walked over to have a closer look and then turned as Adamu came back into the room bearing a decanter and a couple of glasses. "What's an Old Boy of Charterhouse doing working for the security service?" he asked with a smile.

"Ah! that. . . . well Sir, firstly, I hated every minute I spent in that place, no thanks to my father's attempt to keep up with the Joneses. . . or in his case the Dantatas. And second, I'm a police officer, not a spook." He handed Mike a glass. "Cheers, Sir."

"Cheers." Mike took a sip from the glass. "Pretty good. . . Hennessy XO?"

"I'm impressed Sir. When I grow up I want to be like you!" Adamu replied with a laugh.

"You still haven't answered my question," Mike said, sitting back down.

Adamu joined him. "I suppose I've always been a bit of a rebel. I actually wanted to join the Army, but my father absolutely refused to countenance that, so joining the police was a negotiated compromise brokered by my Mum."

"So how long have you been back?"

"Just under nine years . . . been at the Villa for just under two years. Truth be told, I am starting to tire a little of it. Would rather get back to real detective work, so hoping for a posting to EFCC next," Adamu said, referring to the Economic and Financial Crimes Commission.

"Most people might think you mad for actually wanting to leave a cushy job that they'd kill for."

"I'm sure it won't be the last time that I'd be thought mad. Still, if I'm slightly mad, I can think of several people who must be raving lunatics."

"Indeed. Which brings me to why I'm here. You of course know what happened to my family."

Adamu nodded.

"I have my doubts that this was really a failed robbery" Mike went on. "Now that I can start to think straight again, it makes no sense to me. Nothing was taken at the scene, despite the car being full of suitcases and the car was riddled with bullets, which makes no sense if that was what they were after."

Adamu nodded again. "I think you're onto something there. So, if it wasn't a robbery, what was it then?"

"I don't know. . . the obvious explanation is that it was an assassination, but who would want to kill my wife, driver and children?"

"Sir, have you considered the possibility that shooters made a mistake?"

"What do you mean? That they didn't intend to kill?"

"Well, that's one possibility. Another is that they killed the wrong person."

"But who?" . . . Mike's voice tailed off. "My God, they were in my car. Ronke's wouldn't start that morning, so I sent them ahead while I got a mechanic to jump start it and then I followed on to catch up with them."

"So, the question is: Who could have wanted you out of the way?"

Louis Edet House, Abuja, Nigeria

Adamu made his way to a small, un-signposted office towards the rear of the 4th floor of the headquarters of the Nigerian Police. This small section consisted of three or four small offices protected by locks accessible only to a few swipe cards; the officers who worked here never wore uniforms, and they did their own office cleaning, leaving the rubbish in sacks outside the main door every evening. Not that they ever seemed to be off-duty; there always seemed to be light under the door at all hours of the day or night. Adamu let himself in through the main door with a swipe card that never left a slim, black, waterproof wallet, which in turn was never more than arm's length away from him. Having gained access to the suite of offices, he slid aside the door to an innocuous looking key cabinet. Ignoring the keys, he pressed first his left thumb, and then his right ring finger against the sensor concealed on the right side of the cabinet. Turning to his right, he pressed the same two digits against what appeared to be a blank nameplate on the door. The door clicked open with a sigh, and he entered the offices of the small section that was charged with investigating high-level corruption within the police.

Very few policemen knew of their existence, and even fewer of the public. A small, very select group, they went about their business unobtrusively, and had numbered amongst their victims a former inspector-general of police, no less. Not that they'd taken, or even wanted any credit for that coup; they had been content to let the EFCC take that.

"*Fine boy no pimples,*" Bassey greeted Adamu. "You decided to come and see what real life is like outside the rarefied air of the Villa?"

"*How far? Gonorrhoea never kill you yet?*" Adamu replied. Bassey was probably the one person outside his family Adamu was closest to. They'd met on their first day at the Police College and had immediately gelled, perhaps because they were two rebellious young men from privileged backgrounds who had decided to tread a different path. The fact that they also had a similar wicked and wacky sense of humor didn't hurt either. And they were both passionate about what they did; in fact, the unit had partly been their idea.

"*Your papa,*" Bassey replied. The harsh words notwithstanding, they hugged each other with genuine affection.

"How are Ekaette and the kids?"

"They're fine, thanks. Settling into new schools in Atlanta. Can you imagine, I was talking to Etim the other day, the boy was sounding like a Yankee on the phone. I'm having second thoughts about this whole America business o." Bassey had relocated his family to the US about a year before, shortly after joining the unit. His wife Ekaette was a US citizen, and both of their children had been born there; she was now doing a doctorate in criminology at Emory University. Bassey had been relieved to get them out of the country when he had been approached about joining the unit; it seemed he was now having second thoughts.

Adamu smiled humorlessly. "Maybe you'll change your mind about changing your mind when you hear this." He sat down at the desk next to Bassey's and leaned back in the swivel chair, propping his feet up on a corner of the desk. "Do you remember that failed robbery on the airport road a few months ago, when the family of the OP3 Chairman were killed?"

"Yep. Very sad."

"Indeed. Except that it may not have been quite as it seemed." Adamu filled Bassey in on his discussion with Mike. "I need you to do me a favour. I'm travelling with Mr President tomorrow and we'll be out of the country. While I'm away, could you get one of the uniform boys to pull the DPO file on this matter? I think a useful starting point would be seeing what those clowns have or haven't done. In the meantime, I've put out a few feelers among our runners to see what the word on the street is about who was behind this."

"No problem. Will do. Where are you off to . . . anywhere nice?"

Adamu smiled sweetly at Bassey. "Fuck off."

Nnamdi Azikiwe Airport, Abuja, Nigeria one day later

Bassey swung his car into the grounds of the airport police station. As usually seemed to be the case, the yard was littered with several vehicles much the worse for wear after road traffic accidents. He found somewhere to park, climbed out and made his way to the station entrance. A few policemen lounging about on the small raised balcony at the front of the station with mild curiosity, but not a single one moved. So much for an agile and alert force, he thought.

He entered the station proper and approached the counter. He removed his ID card, the one that identified him as being from The Executive Office of the President, and flashed it at the sergeant who was propping his chin up with one hand while picking his teeth with the other. "DCP Inyang. I'm here to see your DPO."

The effect on the sergeant was instantaneous. He leapt to his feet, sending the stool he'd been seated on toppling over with a crash, he tried to salute and at the same time avoid stabbing himself in the eye with the toothpick. He stammered a "welcome sah!" as he emerged from behind the counter with some alacrity. Inviting Bassey to follow him, they walked out past the now more alert policemen on the balcony and across the yard to a small building. Opening the door, he ushered Bassey into a small outer office that had a few chairs along two walls and the obligatory flat screen TV on the third wall, flanked by the equally obligatory portraits of the inspector-general of police and the commissioner of police for the Federal Capital Territory. A door led to an inner office, guarded by a fat policewoman sitting at a desk with an ancient looking computer and some files on it. Taking her cue from the look on the face of the sergeant leading Bassey in, she leapt to her feet and saluted with a booming "morning sah!"

Ignoring the various supplicants sitting around awaiting the DPO's pleasure, the sergeant brusquely instructed the policewoman to go and tell the DPO that "commissioner from HQ" was here to see the DPO. Bassey smiled at his impromptu promotion as the policewoman disappeared into the inner sanctum. In a matter of seconds, the door opened and the DPO him self emerged, saluting as he came.

"Morning sah, you're most welcome. Please I'm sorry that my staff kept you waiting, please come in sah." He stood aside and ushered Bassey into the office, directing him to a sofa in the corner. Bassey dutifully sat down. The DPO pulled up a chair and sat down, not quite opposite Bassey, who could see the man was nervous.

"Mr Ajayi, I'm sure you're wondering why I have come here to see you. Please don't worry, there's no problem, I just need your help with something that we are interested in at the Villa." As Bassey had anticipated, that got the DPO's attention.

"Of course, sah, anything we can do to help."

Bassey paused allowing the man stew for a bit longer. Then he said "I believe you're on your last chance for promotion at the next Board?"

Now Bassey really had the DPO's full attention. "Y-y- yes sah," he stammered.

Bassey paused again. "There was an accident on the airport expressway about 3, 4 months ago. It followed a failed robbery attempt early in the morning. Four people died, including two children,"

"I remember the case sah, very sad. I think we released the vehicle to the insurance people only last week, once we completed our investigations. I even took a personal . . ."

Bassey cut him off. "I need the case file."

"Right away sah. I will go and get it for you now." He started to get up, and sat down again abruptly in response to Bassey's waved command.

"Not now. I am going to leave now. In about an hour or so, send that fat woman outside to get 4 or 5 case files, including the one I want. At 5 o'clock this afternoon sharp, be standing in front of the Federal High Court building with all five case files in a briefcase. Somebody will meet you there and greet you by asking whether the promotion board has sat yet. Hand the briefcase to him and leave immediately. If we need any more information, I will get in touch with you. It goes without saying that you will discuss this matter with nobody at all, not even with that married woman you're sleeping with and building a house for in Lokoja."

The DPO recoiled, as Bassey had intended. "How, I mean, but" — Bassey smiled again mirthlessly, got up and left.

Louis Edet House, Abuja, Nigeria, five days later

"The whole thing stinks to high heaven," Bassey said, as Adamu flicked through the case file. "First, the timing – what self-respecting armed robber operates at 7 a.m.? Second, having decided to do so, why leave without taking anything, when you have the worldly goods, if not the vehicle, of your victims at your mercy? Third, according to the eyewitness statements in the file, the robbers made no attempt to stop the victims' vehicle, but opened fire as soon as they came alongside. If the object was to steal the vehicle, why disable it at the scene by riddling the engine with bullets? Fourth, in order to reach the Prado the victims were travelling in, the robbers had driven past and ignored at least two other Prados and at least one Lexus and one Mercedes jeep. No, this was no robbery; this was an assassination."

Adamu looked up. "I agree . . . but why these victims?"

"You said it yourself, they weren't the intended victims. Your friend was."

Adamu shut the file and leaned back. "So, motive, means and opportunity?"

"Your problem, my friend, not mine. I've done my bit, I'm sure even your presidential champagne lifestyle hasn't so rotted your brains that you can't figure the rest of it out."

"Dan bura uba."

Igore, Nigeria, three days later

Akin sat in his office in the governor's office complex feeling deflated and miserable. The sign at the entrance to his suite of offices next door to the governor's proclaimed him to be The Hon Chief of Staff to His Excellency the Executive Governor of Kauru State, but, for some reason, Akin did not feel any great sense of elation or accomplishment. True, it had been a hard fought (and occasionally bloody) campaign, and the first flush of victory had indeed been sweet, but all that was left now was a huge sense of anti-climax. Yes, he now had his own security detail and convoy, and could feed and grow fat on the largesse from the hordes of people seeking the governor's favour for one thing or another, but none of that seemed to matter now. Truth be told, Akin, despite all the bluster and swagger, was scared. He'd seen close up just how dirty elective politics could be, and just how ruthless Big Man, the new governor and his backers could be. And then the deaths of Ronke and the twins. He'd known instinctively that Mike had been the target, and in that case that Big Man had to have been involved in some way. Yes, there was a lot at stake, and yes, these people played for keeps, and yes, he'd tried to warn Mike . . . but never in his wildest dreams did he think it would come to this. He noticed that the matter of Mike's family's deaths had never even been brought up once by the Big Man, which was just as chilling.

Akin remembered the awful grief he felt at the funeral, made worse by a sense of guilt that he may have partially been responsible. Despite his best efforts, he'd never been able to subsume that guilt in any of the several different self-justifying ways he had tried. And now, he'd never be able to . . . because now he knew.

He had been having a quick chat with Big Man in his office the day before on the upcoming budget. Big Man had been in a bit of a hurry as he was running late for a courtesy call on the Emir, and hadn't really been listening. Akin had to be content with a "Let's discuss further when I get back" and with that Big Man swept out of the office. Akin was just about to follow when he felt an urgent need to pee, and decided to use Big Man's personal bathroom adjacent to his office; after all, there had to be some perks of this job, right? He'd just been about to flush the loo when he heard voices from the office, and realised with some surprise that Big Man had come back into the office. Wondering what had made Big Man come back, Akin stopped to listen, and was surprised to hear the sheer fury in Big Man's voice as he asked "What the hell are you doing here? I thought I told you to only see me in the guest house?"

Akin was even more surprised to hear Casablanca's voice — what was that thug doing here? He soon found out. *"Alarm don blow o.* You know those boys that did the job on Anako? Well, I told them to lay low for a while and not return here until things cooled down. I haven't used them for any job since they came back to punish them small, but it seems they've been doing their own operations to make extra money. They tried to rob a petrol station just outside Oshogbo, but unfortunately for them some mobile policemen were passing and engaged them. Three of them were killed, including one of the boys who did the job, and two arrested. The only one who got away was the other boy, Morocco."

"So why are you telling me this? Isn't that what we pay

you for, to take care of shit like that? Go and sort it out, my friend, and don't ever come to this place again! Now get out."

Akin waited until he was sure that Big Man and his unwanted guest had left, then quietly slipped out of the toilet and into the corridor and returned to his office. He locked the door and sat down, sweaty and shaking. What was that Casablanca had said? The boys who did the Anako job? Holy shit, what had he got himself into?

And so, Akin sat, thinking through his options. They did not seem particularly great right now. He now could not console himself with the thought that maybe, just maybe, Big Man had not been involved in the deaths of Mike's wife and children. Now that he knew the truth, he realised that his best bet was for Big Man not know that he, Akin, knew the truth. That way, he could hang around for a few months, then cite some spurious health reason, resign and get the hell out of this dream turned nightmare. Yes, that was it . . . or so he thought.

Ikirun, Nigeria

Morocco was now as scared as he had ever been in his life. The Oshogbo robbery had gone wrong right from the start. He had never been keen on the Oshogbo crew in the first place, but Razor had insisted that he had worked with them in the past on a few successful operations. Well, so much for that. God knows where those bloody policemen came from, but the rubbish weapons the Oshogbo boys supplied had rendered the gang almost impotent to fight back — Morocco still had nightmares about the AK47 jamming in his hands as he tried to escape from the petrol station. How he got away was a mystery to him, given the volume of fire the police had sent his way; the fact that he was pretty much unscathed, save from a few scratches and bruises from the thorny bushes he had struggled through was clearly the result of divine intervention from the God that he had long ago abandoned. He skirted a few compounds, stopping only to exchange his torn clothes for an Ankara *buba* and *sokoto* that some thoughtful person had put out to dry. The robbery had netted a few thousand naira before those bloody policemen intervened, which had come in handy to get himself away from Oshogbo and buy a cheap phone with which to call Casablanca. That the aforesaid Casablanca had not been helpful was an understatement of gargantuan proportions; in essence, Morocco was on his own. Since Casablanca's coterie of thugs and thieves was all he had known since running away from home in Auchi at the age of 13, and since the last he had seen of his mentor Razor had involved a substantial quantity of his brains spattered across the forecourt of the petrol station they had tried to rob, there was really nowhere to turn; he would have to survive on his wits.

Morocco told himself he needed to calm down and think. He may not have had much formal education, but he was by no means a complete fool, and he had learned street smarts in his years with Casablanca's mob. He checked how much money he had left: just over 32,000 naira. Where could he go, and how much would that cost him? Igore was out of the question; he would be dead within minutes if he set foot on Casablanca's turf. Ikirun was too close to both Oshogbo and Igore for comfort, so he could not stay here. He thought for a moment, then stopped a passing *okada* and asked to be taken to the Ikirun motor park. That was the sort of environment he had grown up in, and he felt comfortable there; he might also be able to work out what his next move should be from there.

He alighted from the *okada* a few minutes later, and wandered into the motor park, listening to the conductors shouting out various destinations. He looked around for the inevitable beer parlour, entered and sat himself in a corner. The young woman serving seemed vaguely familiar, but female company was the last thing on Morocco's mind right now. He asked for a small stout and a cigarette and settled back to think.

CHAPTER 7

Abuja, Nigeria, two days later

MIKE STARED AT ADAMU AND BASSEY WITH something approaching disbelief. He had been in the middle of sorting out the stuff in the Maitama flat, determining what he wanted to keep and what he needed to get rid of, when Adamu had called from a number Mike wasn't familiar with and asked if he could come over and see him with 'one of my colleagues'. Mike had readily agreed, and it was a while after he put the phone down that it suddenly struck him that Adamu hadn't asked him for the address. He was about to try the number Chike had given him for Adamu when the buzzer rang, and he let Adamu and his colleague in. After introductions were done, and he had cleared some space for them to sit down amidst the clutter, he listened as they had walked him through what they'd found so far, and their initial conclusions.

"So, Sir, you see that the key issue here is to work out who could have wanted you out of the way, and why. I realise that this may be easier said than done, but we need your help if we're to get to the bottom of this," Adamu concluded.

"For what it's worth, I think it may be an idea to start with your OP3 role . . . any thoughts?" Bassey asked.

Mike got up and walked over to the window. He stared down at the swimming pool area for a minute, then turned and faced his two visitors. "The only thing I can think of is the Lagos Ports business that's been in the papers recently."

Mike ran through the story of the visit from Mrs Adebisi,

the subsequent conversation with Akin regarding Big Man's interest in the matter, and his surprise to read in the papers that although the company that submitted the worst of the four bids, Big Man's coterie had been awarded the concession in Akin's absence from OP3. "I have to tell you that I can't believe that either Akin or Big Man could have wanted me dead just because of the Port concession deal."

Bassey smiled weakly. "Sir, you'd be surprised about what Adamu and I are capable of believing."

Mike came and sat back down. "So, what are we going to do?"

Adamu leaned forward. "May I suggest that what you are going to do is to submit your resignation from OP3 to the Presidency tomorrow, and request permission to serve your notice period as terminal leave? That way, whoever may have been gunning for you will be reassured that you will no longer pose a threat to them, which will protect you. Once you've done that, keep a low profile; it might be best if you perhaps left the country for a while to rest and recuperate. In the meantime, we will make a few enquiries about this Ports deal. Please don't discuss this with anyone Sir, and we really do mean anyone."

"How do we keep in touch? Can I reach you on the number Chike gave me for you? I noticed that you called from a different number earlier."

"You can always reach me on that number. I suggest that you send a text every Monday and Friday at 9 p.m. Abuja time, and one of us will get back to you. Please, I can't overemphasize the value of discretion — these people, whoever they are, have demonstrated a willingness to use lethal force once already."

As Adamu and Bassey drove away from Mike's flat, both men were initially silent, each preoccupied with their thoughts. Eventually, Adamu broke the silence.

"You know, if Big Man was indeed involved in this, we can't touch him right now."

"Maybe not, but we can still make enquiries, can't we? I think we need to dig around into this Ports thing a bit more, but we need a front—it's not really our bailiwick. Ideally, someone at EFCC— didn't you work with someone there on the former IG's case?" That had happened before Bassey joined the unit.

"I'll sort that out. Meantime, I think we need to check out the Adebisi woman and this Akin fellow; they are likely to be the weak links in this chain, if indeed there's a chain. I think you need to lean on the Airport DPO a bit more; those cops always know most, if not all the villains operating on their patch. Let's see if we can shake something out about who did the actual hit."

"Leave that with me. I haven't been to Lagos for a while, so I'll go and check out the Adebisi woman too. Will you look into the Akin fellow?"

Adamu looked sideways at Bassey with a teasing grin. "For somebody who didn't want to have anything to do with this, you've certainly slipped very easily into allocating troops to tasks mode." Bassey's reply was unprintable.

The Presidential Villa, Abuja, Nigeria, the next day

As Mike waited to get through security, he felt his jacket pocket to make sure the sealed white envelope containing his resignation was there. He had composed the letter several times in his head as he tossed and turned in bed the previous night after Adamu and Bassey left his flat. He had been inclined to resign from government service anyway, but last night's conversation had made up his mind. He eventually gave up on sleep, got out of bed and powered up his laptop. He went through a few drafts before he settled on a form of words he was happy with. Having printed off a couple of copies, he sealed them in separate envelopes, and returned to bed where, to his surprise, he fell promptly asleep. Thankfully he had set an alarm to get up and call the president's chief of staff's office to try and squeeze in an appointment for today, which he had eventually managed to do. So here he was, possibly for the last time. He eventually got through security and made his way to the chief of staff's office. A flunky invited him to take a seat. Eventually, he was ushered into the chief of staff's office.

"Mike, welcome back. I hope things are settling down for you after the terrible tragedy. I hope you saw the condolence letter from Mr President and also from myself?"

"Yes Sir, I did. My apologies that I have not written back to formally acknowledge, but as you can imagine, I haven't been in the best of shape lately. In fact, that's why I'm here Sir." Mike drew the envelope from his jacket pocket and handed it to the chief of staff. "I don't think I am in a position to carry on at OP3, so I hope that you will convey my letter of resignation to Mr President, with my gratitude for the opportunity to serve."

The chief of staff opened the envelope and quickly read the brief letter. Replacing it in the envelope, he looked up. "Are you sure you want to do this? We think you've been doing a great job at OP3 and we would be sorry to lose you. I know it's been a difficult time for you, and you've been away on compassionate leave, but I'm sure Mr President would be happy to authorize an extension of your compassionate leave, if that would help." He sounded sincere.

Mike shook his head. "Thank you Sir, but my mind is made up. I would appreciate it if I could be allowed to serve out my notice period as my terminal leave starting tomorrow, so that the search for my replacement can start straightaway."

"That should not be a problem. I'm sure Mr President would want to thank you in person; I'll try to arrange a meeting before the end of your terminal leave. If we need to, I hope we can seek your advice on your replacement?"

"Absolutely Sir."

Lokoja-Abuja Road, Nigeria, one day later

The idea had come to Morocco in the beer parlour at Ikirun. He had finally worked out why the girl serving him had seemed familiar; she was the spitting image of the girl he'd spent the night with in Suleija before he and Razor had headed off in a hurry all those weeks ago. Now what was her name again? Patience, that was it. She'd actually been good company, and wild in bed to boot. He was sure he could find his way back to the hotel they'd stayed at, and it would be a good place to lay low while he took stock and re-grouped. He'd gone back outside and haggled with the conductor of the minibus going to Abuja to try and secure a bargain fare; after all, until he could replenish his funds, most likely by robbing someone, he'd have to watch his spending. He was now squashed in the middle row of the minibus headed to Abuja. What a shit life, he thought.

Hotel Chelsea, Abuja, Nigeria, later the same day

The Airport DPO was sweating despite the air-conditioning in the modest hotel room. Ever since he had taken Bassey's phone call earlier in the day instructing him to meet him in room 319 of this hotel, he'd been in a bit of a panic, for that was exactly the same room in the same hotel that he used for his trysts with the married woman that Bassey had referred to at their first meeting. What else did the bastard know, he wondered? He had dutifully turned up as instructed and was admitted to the room by a smiling Bassey.

"Please sit down, Mr Ajayi, and make yourself at home; after all, you are familiar with this room, are you not? Bassey indicated that the DPO sit on the bed. The smile was still in place on Bassey's lips, but if you looked carefully, there was little mirth in his face. "Oh, and by the way, your case files are in the briefcase."

The DPO sat down as instructed. Bassey sat himself down on a chair and looked at the DPO with distaste. "There are people in the Villa who are most unhappy about the shoddy investigation you and your people did into the matter I came to see you about the other day. They want to crucify you, but I have held them at bay for now." Bassey paused for a second, then carried on. "I hope you have worked out by now that I know enough about you to not only end your sad and sorry career in the police, but to send you to jail for a very long time. Whether that happens or not is up to you. I need you to do something for me; if you deliver, all will be forgiven and forgotten. If not—" Bassey let the implied threat hang in the air.

"Sir, whatever you need, just let me know. I swear, I will deliver."

"Well, we'll see. I want to know who carried out that attack. Somebody, somewhere knows, and since it happened on your patch, I need you to find that somebody. In exactly one week from today, meet me back here, and God bless you if you come empty-handed. All I need from you is a name or names, and where they can be found. I don't want you and your baboons charging around and screwing things up. Is that clear?"

"Yes sah. I won't let you down sah, I swear."

Nnamdi Azikiwe airport, Abuja, Nigeria, later the same day

Shit flows downhill, so the DPO was determined that if he had to thrash his men to death to get the information Bassey wanted, so be it. He returned to his station in a foul mood, and summoned his three most senior subordinate officers into his office.

"Which of you was the IPO on the failed robbery on the airport road a few months ago where that woman and her children were killed?"

One of the inspectors timidly raised a hand. "Sir, I was the one."

"I should have known," the DPO said, glaring at the unfortunate man. "Well you fucked up, and you and your fellow idiots are going to have to clean up your mess. I want you to go and quietly quiz all your informants as to who did that operation. And notice I said quietly. I don't want any of your *agbero* behaviour on this one. Just get me the names and locations of the bastards within the next 48 hours. If you fail, you and I will wear the same trouser in this station. Now get out of my sight!"

Suleija, Nigeria, early morning the next day

Morocco woke up feeling slightly disoriented. It took him a while to work out where he was, the process being made easier when he felt Patience's plump warmth next to him. It had actually been easier than he's expected to locate her — he'd walked into the hotel, and there she was, sitting at the bar. The reunion had been made even sweeter by the fact that he'd managed to relieve one of his fellow passengers of about 50,000 naira, which they had foolishly left unattended in a bag, and which he had managed to filch as the passengers disembarked in Abuja.

A few drinks and joints had been followed by some mind-blowing sex . . . things were looking up. Or perhaps not.

A few doors away, the hotel proprietor awoke to the unwelcome sight of one of the inspectors from the airport police station shaking him awake. The inspector was not in uniform and appeared to be having an acute attack of sense of humor failure. "*Oya, get up, get up and wear ya cloth*. We need to talk." The same scenario was being repeated in a number of homes, hotels, brothels and drug dens across the district; informers were being leant on in response to the DPO's edict of the day before. In exchange for being left alone to run his cannabis farms and his brothel, he occasionally passed the odd tidbit to the police on top of the protection money he paid. The proprietor sleepily got to his feet and threw on a few clothes.

"*But oga, you no dey usually come our side . . . na wetin happen?*"

"I need some information, and I need it quickly. Some boys did an operation near the airport a few months ago. DPO needs to know who did it."

"*Haba, oga, how I go know dat kin tin? Na hotel be my business na?*"

"*Ehen? Na rat, abi na goat dey sleep for your hotel? No be all these boys wey dey operate around here be your customer? My friend, please don't waste my time with foolish talk for dis kin early morning o.*"

"*Walahi, oga, I never hear anything about dat operation o. I . . .* his voice tailed off.

The inspector's ears perked up. "*Wetin you hear?*"

The proprietor made a quick risk-benefit analysis in his head, and decided that keeping in with the local police was far more in his long-term interests than loyalty to a couple of transient thugs.

"*Some two boys bin dey around at the time of that operation. Na early morning dat day dem komot, I no see dem again till one of dem show again last night. Im dey hotel now with one of my girls.*"

"*Wetin be de guy name?*"

"*Na Morocco dem dey call am.*"

"*The girl nko?*"

"*Patience.*"

"What of the other guy?"

"*Oga, I no remember o . . .* something like Nacet blade." His brow furrowed as he struggled to remember, then it came to him. "*Razor, dat na de other boy name.*"

"Very good. *Watch the guy for me, and call me if e be like say e wan komot.* Meanwhile, keep your mouth shut, you hear?"

"No problem, *oga.*"

Hilton Hotel, Abuja, Nigeria, later the same day

Bassey watched the DPO emerge from the hotel building to the pool side, scanning around anxiously till he spotted Bassey. He hurried across, puffing slightly. Bassey waved him to a chair, and beckoned a waiter over.

"Will you join me in a beer?" "No, thank you Sir, water is fine."

Bassey nodded to the waiter and smiled across the table at the DPO. "I gather you have some news?"

"Yes Sir, my boys—" Bassey motioned him to stop as the waiter approached with a bottle of water, some ice and a fresh bowl of peanuts on a tray. He waited until the waiter served the water and departed, then motioned to the DPO to continue.

"My boys went out first thing this morning, and one of the teams in Suleija have come up with something that I thought you would want to hear straightaway." He quickly filled Bassey in with the details of the suspect, known as Morocco.

"I take it you have someone maintaining surveillance?"

The DPO looked taken aback. "Sir, but I thought you said that we should keep it quiet."

"I did. And do you usually conduct surveillance with a marching band?"

"No Sir, I will get on to it right away."

"You will do no such thing. Make sure your people are in hourly contact with the hotel manager and are fully updated on this fellow's whereabouts at all times. If he gets away, heads will roll . . . yours first."

Bassey paused for a moment. "I will call you in a couple of hours with further instructions."

Louis Edet House, Abuja, Nigeria, later that evening

Bassey and Adamu were having a council of war. Truth be told, they had not expected a breakthrough quite this early from shaking down the DPO, but they seemed to have gotten lucky. The question now was how best to proceed.

"I think we need to lift this guy quickly, but quietly," Adamu was saying. "If we can get our hands on him before his people know he's out of circulation, he could be a rich source of information about the hit on Mike's family."

"Fine, but how? We're freelancing on this one, so we're limited in the assets we can draw on and keep our fingerprints off this operation. As it is, Oga's starting to sniff around as to what exactly it is I'm up to right now. And after we lift this creature and extract what we need from him, what do we do with him – let him go again?"

Adamu gave Bassey an old-fashioned look. "Sufficient unto the day is the evil thereof," he intoned solemnly. Thankfully, their boss, commissioner of police James Aloysius was that rarest of creatures—a Nigerian boss who did not mind getting his hands dirty and getting out and actually doing the same sorts of things his very small team did. He was as often to be found out on the ground running down leads and following up investigations, as he was to be behind his desk in their small and very secret headquarters. A small, unremarkable-looking spare man in his late forties, he could pass for being twenty years younger, causing many crooks over the years to fatally underestimate him.

He had handpicked his small team personally, and tended to give them freedom to manoeuvre, within reason. "I have a friend who's an officer in the Brigade of Guards. He owes me a favour, and I'm sure I can rely on him to be discreet. If he gets his people to lift this Morocco fellow, we can hold him in one of the safe houses outside town and question him there. Depending on how cooperative he proves to be, we can either let him go, or return him to the loving care of your DPO friend. As for *Oga* James, leave him to me; we'll cross that bridge when we come to it."

Aguiyi-Ironsi Cantonment, Abuja, Nigeria, Later that evening

Major Bitrus Temlong looked exactly like what he was: a seasoned, battle-hardened professional soldier. Small, wiry and erect, he spoke in short, staccato bursts. If Adamu and Bassey showing up in his Married Quarter in the Cantonment at that time of night had surprised him, he didn't show it. He politely invited them in and offered them drinks. He sat quietly listening to Adamu outline what it was they wanted from him. Once Adamu was done, Major Temlong looked at him expressionlessly for a minute, and then said, "You do realise what you're asking me to do could cost me my career?"

Adamu nodded, but otherwise made no reply.

"More importantly, it could also cost my boys their careers and livelihood too. I won't do that without asking them. I need to speak to a couple of my boys. Please wait." He excused himself, and Adamu and Bassey could hear him speaking in Hausa next door, presumably on the phone. He returned in a couple of minutes, and sat down again. "My sergeant major and one of my platoon commanders will be here shortly. When they arrive, please tell them exactly what you have told me; after that we will have a discussion among ourselves and only then will I give you an answer. More wine, anyone?"

Sergeant Major Dan Bauchi and Lt Akinwande were cut from the same cloth as their boss, save that the sergeant major was older and the lieutenant younger than Major Temlong; it was also clear that they both held him in high esteem. Major Temlong invited Adamu and Bassey to repeat to his colleagues what they had told him earlier, which they did. Once done, the three soldiers stepped outside, leaving the two police officers on their own indoors.

"What do you think?" Bassey asked Adamu.

Adamu shrugged. "Bitrus has always had an independent

mind, but I really think the game changer here will be what the sergeant major thinks."

"If I live to be a hundred, I'll never understand these military boys and how they think," Bassey replied. "Still, I have to say your major friend has excellent taste in red wine . . . pass the bottle before you finish it."

The door opened and they were surprised to see it was the sergeant major on his own. He stared at Adamu and Bassey in turn, then said, very slowly, "Please tell me the truth. Why exactly do you want us to arrest this thug for you? We are soldiers, not policemen, which is what I suspect you are. So why not arrest him yourself? If you want us to have anything to do with this crazy idea, I need to know the truth."

Adamu and Bassey looked at each other for a minute, then both nodded at the same time. Adamu leaned forward and cleared his throat. "Sergeant major, everything I told Major Temlong and you is true, but you're partially right—it wasn't the whole truth. My colleague and I are both police officers, but not the regular kind. We are both members of a special unit that investigates high-level corruption. As far as we know, this case is one of straightforward multiple murder, which is not what we do. We both think there is a strong possibility that the reason for the murders was high-level corruption, but at this stage, we do not want to alert the people we think may be behind it, nor do we want our fellow police officers to know we're working on this matter—that's why we've approached you for help." He stopped and sat back.

Bassey looked on admiringly—he'd just seen a master class in obfuscation, half-truths and false trails, delivered with the sincerity of the Sermon on the Mount. In any event, Sgt Major Dan Bauchi seemed satisfied. He nodded, got up and went outside to rejoin his officers. A few minutes later, all three returned.

"How exactly do you want us to help?"

Suleija, Nigeria, early hours of the next day

Morocco never knew what hit him. The interval between the door of his room being kicked off its hinges, through seeing a masked figure and feeling a weapon being pressed to the side of his head, to being handcuffed, hooded and thrown into the back of a van seemed like a few seconds. He felt horribly exposed, not surprisingly perhaps, given that he was stark naked save for the hood over his head. Worse, the only thing his captors said to him was a promise to shoot him in the head if he uttered a word—given the calmly sincere way the threat was uttered, he was not inclined to put their resolve to the test. So he lay mute for the entire journey.

After what seemed like an eternity, the van slowed down and stopped. Still without saying anything to him, his abductors removed him from the vehicle and marched him over some rough ground and into a building. He was led into a room, pushed into a chair and felt his arms and legs being lashed tightly to the chair. He heard his captors leave, still without saying a word and the door closed behind them. The shock of capture now really set in. Just as he was pondering what horrible fate was in store for him, the hood over was abruptly removed. Morocco squinted against the sudden light.

"My friend, you have been brought here because I need something from you. I am going to get it, for sure. The only thing that is not sure is how much pain you are going to suffer before I get it; that is up to you. I suggest that it is in your interests to cooperate quickly."

Morocco was now quite literally pissing himself with fear. This was nothing like the straightforward thuggery and brutality of the motor park and area boys he was used to. Truth be told, like most thugs and bullies, he was a bit of a coward. The fact that he could not see who was talking to him, and the calm way this man was talking, just made it worse. All of which Bassey was perfectly aware of, which was why he was doing this before the shock of capture wore off and Morocco regained his wits. Just to persuade Morocco that he really was in serious shit, Bassey ostentatiously cocked a pistol just behind Morocco's left ear. "Am I making myself clear?" Morocco nodded dumbly.

"Good. Now tell me who sent you to do that operation on the airport road a few months ago."

CHAPTER 8

Abuja, Nigeria, later the same day

MIKE HAD BEEN ABOUT TO STEP OUT OF HIS FLAT TO head to his travel agent's office when he'd received a call on his phone from a number he didn't recognise. He ignored it, but the caller was persistent. Eventually he got a text from the same number saying "It's not 9 p.m. on Monday or Friday, but answer the phone anyway." Mike realised it was Adamu, and answered the phone the next time it rang.

"Sir, we need to talk. Please meet me at Shoprite near the Yar'Adua centre at 3 p.m. this afternoon. If possible, please take a taxi or car hire."

"Sure. What's up?"

"See you at 3 p.m. Sir." Adamu rang off.

Mike had been almost late for the rendezvous, despite arriving early. As he often tended to do, he'd lost track of time whilst browsing in a bookstore, and realised with a start that he needed to get a move on if he wasn't going to be late. Just as he was leaving the bookshop, his phone rang, this time from a withheld number. "Hello?"

"Sir, please use the side entrance when you exit the bookshop. When you do, look to your left. There's a grey Toyota Camry with Jigawa State licence plates — I'm in it."

Adamu picked up Mike, and they'd headed towards Apo. Adamu didn't seem in the mood to talk, so they sat in silence on the drive. Eventually, after what seemed like a circuitous journey, they'd pulled off the road into a small estate in Apo;

Mike was not particularly surprised when Bassey opened the door to the flat and let them in.

The flat bore all the signs of what had once been a family home that was now a bachelor pad. Mike noticed the family photos on a side table that showed Bassey, presumably his wife, and two little boys who looked like they might be twins. Bassey followed Mike's gaze, then saw the quizzical look in his eyes and nodded. "Yes Sir, I'm a *Baba'beji* too. . . and that's partly why we're going to get the bastards who did this."

Bassey cleared away the magazines, books, and newspapers that covered the chairs and sofa. "Please sit down. Sorry I can't offer you guys any food apart from some leftover take-away in the fridge, but I can offer you drinks . . . wine, beer, spirits? I have some good rum I bought in duty-free on my way back from seeing the family."

"A cold beer would be good. Thanks." Mike replied. "Make that two," Adamu added.

Beers in hand, the duo sat down. Bassey said, "Sir, we think we may have found one of the two guys who carried out the attack on your family. As we suspected, you were the target, but it seems that the goons exceeded their instructions; they were meant to frighten, and not kill you; of course, because your wife's car had broken down that morning, they, and not you, were in your vehicle. The object of the whole exercise was the Ports concession, as you suspected. A character called Casablanca, who is a notorious hoodlum in Igore, and is known to be a political associate of your previous boss, the former minister and now the governor of Kauru State, Big Man, sent the thugs. What we don't yet know is who else was involved, but we're now trying to rundown the leads the chap we caught has given us. By the way, the other hoodlum involved met his end a few days ago in a hail of police bullets during a foiled robbery."

It didn't escape Mike's notice that Bassey had spoken in

general terms, and he suspected there was more to the story that he was not being told; he could live with that, as long as Ronke and the twins' killers got their comeuppance.

Adamu took up the talking. "Sir, I'm afraid that one of the people we'll need to look at closely is your friend Akin, who, as I'm sure you're aware, is now the chief of staff to Big Man. We may need your help to get close to him, but we're aware that could be difficult for you."

Mike sat in silence for a few moments. He was struggling to come to terms with the fact that his family had been killed by accident; the news reopened the old wounds of guilt that *he* should have been in the jeep that day, not them. He felt the bile come up in his throat, and he took a couple of deep breaths before he felt able to respond. "Gentlemen, I would like to thank you very much for all your efforts on my behalf," he began. He swallowed again, then resumed. "I can't lie that this is reopening recent wounds, but I want you to know one thing: I would go to hell and back to bring the people who killed my family to justice."

There was silence for a few minutes. Then Adamu spoke again. "We understand, Sir. Here's what we would like you to do."

Igore, Nigeria, later that evening

Akin was having a rare evening at home. He sat in front of the TV, staring at a football match that he was not really concentrating on. All he could think about was how he was going to safely negotiate his exit from the situation he was in. He had no illusions as to what would befall him, or worse, his family, if Big Man and his cohorts ever became aware that he knew what he knew, and ever suspected him of no longer being 'one of us'. Akin wondered bitterly if he had ever been truly been 'one of them' — too late now for recriminations.

The beeping of the phone brought him back to the present.

Glancing idly at it, he saw it was a text message from Mike. Involuntarily, his heart skipped a beat. With shaky hands, he reached for the phone and

> *Your Excellency, how now? Trust you're fully settled into your exalted role. Long time. I'm likely to be passing through Igore next week Tuesday – shipping some stuff from the flat in Abuja down to Ronke's parents in Ijebu. Would be good to catch up if you have time in your busy schedule (LOL). Rgds, Mike.*

Akin read and re-read the message several times. The last thing he needed now was to see the person who was such a central figure in his current feelings of misery and guilt. He thought about fobbing Mike off with some story about needing to be out of town with Big Man, but realised that he was struggling to come up with a form of words that sounded credible. He did not know that including Ronke's name in the text had been a deliberate ploy by Mike, Adamu and Bassey to make it harder for Akin to avoid the meeting.

Falling neatly into the trap, he texted back: *Sure bro. Call when you get in. See u then.*

A few days later, Mike waited in the Barat Kauru Hotel for Akin to arrive. He started to fiddle again with the lapel badge in the form of the Nigerian flag, which was in fact a microphone that Adamu and Bassey had insisted he wear, then stopped himself; that was why the meeting was at the hotel, and not the governor's office, to avoid having to go through a security screen. Recording in a public place with ambient noise would be more challenging, but it was imperative that the conversation being recorded be kept secret. At a table a few feet away, Bassey sat nursing a beer, seemingly engrossed in something on his iPad, with earphones plugged in; even Mike was unaware that they were directly linked to the microphone he was wearing, and that the iPad would be recording every word of his conversation with Akin. Mike glanced at his watch again. As usual, Akin was late. Mike was debating whether to order another drink when Akin appeared, with a couple of flunkies in tow. He scanned the bar, spotted Mike and walked over; to Mike's relief, the flunkies stayed by the door. He had wondered how he would feel seeing Akin again and knowing what he now knew, but was surprised how empty he felt.

"Bro, how now? Good to see you."

"Akin, *Your Excellency*, good to see you too." Mike replied, forcing himself to strike the right sort of teasing, jovial tone that was the norm for them . . . had been the norm for them.

"Leave that matter. How are you coping?"

"*Wetin man go do?* Life must go on. *E no easy sha.*"

"I can imagine. *Pele o*," Akin sat down and waved a waiter across.

Mike studied his erstwhile friend as he ordered a large brandy and Red Bull. There was something not quite right, and for a bit he struggled to work out what it was. Then it struck him – Akin seemed very nervous, and was actually sweating a fair bit even in this air-conditioned bar. Now wasn't that interesting?

"You know I've resigned from OP3?"

"Yeah, I heard. What are your plans now?"

"Not sure. Going to take some time out and get my head straight, probably going to travel out for a while, then I might see what openings there are. Who knows, I might come and ask you to beg Big Man for a job with his friend Mrs. Adebisi at the Ports Authority," Mike delivered this with a smile.

Clearly Akin did not appreciate the joke. If he was nervous before, he was certainly spooked now, spilling some of his drink as he raised it to his mouth with somewhat shaky hands. "I swear, I didn't have anything to do with that . . . I was just the messenger boy."

"Who said you did? As I recall, you said you were trying to protect me . . . maybe I should have listened to you."

"Look, I'm really sorry about what happened... I had no

idea ... I could see that Big Man was really keen to make sure that Adolak got the concession, but ..." Akin seemed to realise he was babbling dangerously, and stopped abruptly.

"What exactly did you mean when you said I was in over my head?"

Akin was in full retreat now. "I don't recall ever saying anything like that. Some things are just better left alone." He took another gulp of his drink.

Mike decided to try another tack. "How's the family? he asked.

Akin replied, "They're fine, thanks."

"My warmest regards to them. I can't tell you what I would give to have my family again."

To everyone's amazement, Akin's eyes welled up, and then he started to sob. Mike looked on initially in amazement, swiftly followed embarrassment. He looked round to see whether anyone had noticed, and caught Bassey's eye, who discreetly motioned to him to press on with the conversation. Mike fumbled in his pocket for a handkerchief, which he passed over to Akin.

"Mike, I'm so sorry, I didn't realise they were prepared to go that far." Akin was mumbling now.

Mike leaned forward and spoke quietly. "Akin, I'm not sure what you mean, but maybe we should go somewhere a bit more private to talk?"

A few minutes later, they were in a room upstairs in the hotel that Mike had hastily gone to reception to book. Akin seemed determined to unburden his soul, and his words flooded out as he recounted the conversation he had overheard from Big Man's private bathroom the previous week. Mike sat in silence as Akin confirmed that Casablanca had indeed despatched Razor and Morocco on the operation that led to Ronke and the twins being killed, but here was the first piece of evidence that tied Big Man directly to it. He thought for a moment, then made a snap judgement—Bassey needed to hear this. He pulled out his phone and sent a text to the number Bassey had given him. *Pls come to rm 242 asap.*

In a matter of minutes, there was a tap on the door. Akin looked up with a start. Mike motioned reassuringly and walked to the door to let Bassey in.

"Who's this?" Akin asked Mike.

"A friend of mine," came the reply. "Please tell him what you just told me."

Akin got up. "Look, I have to go, I have a meeting at the Governor's Office that—"

Bassey's voice was like a rasp as he cut him off. "Your boss may have constitutional immunity, but you do not. If you don't want to be arrested here and now for being an accessory to mass murder, please sit down and shut up."

Both Mike and Akin looked stunned. Akin sat back down.

"Good. Please forgive my tone, but I am actually doing you a favour. How long do you think you'd survive, even in police custody if your boss and Casablanca knew that you knew what they'd been up to?" Bassey could see that the thought hadn't occurred to either of the other two men in the room, although he could see Mike looking at him somewhat quizzically. Bassey ignored the look and sat down facing Akin.

"You know, and we now know, that Big Man is at best guilty of conspiracy to inflict grievous bodily harm, and at worst of conspiracy to murder. We also know that you could be indicted as an accessory before and after the fact. What we don't know for sure is *why* there is a conspiracy, and that's where you come in; you're going to help us find out. If you cooperate with us, I see no reason your name should ever be mentioned in connection with this matter.

If you don't … well you'll have to take your chances either with the criminal justice system, or with the compassion of Big Man and Casablanca. Your call."

Akin stared at Mike. "Who is this guy?"

Mike looked at Bassey, and then looked away. This was Bassey's to answer. Bassey sighed and then, in a kindlier voice said "I'm a police officer attached to Force CID, and I am investigating these murders." He saw no need to burden Akin with the truth.

"And if I cooperate, you'll make sure I don't get roped in?"

"Yep."

"Okay, what do you need me to do?"

Louis Edet House, Abuja, Nigeria, two days later

James Aloysius leaned back in his swivel chair and eyed Adamu and Bassey expressionlessly. He heard them out as they set out the whole story thus far, occasionally interrupting to seek clarification. For a while he didn't say anything, and the other two knew better than to break the silence. Eventually, in a voice surprisingly deep for so slight a man, he asked the question Adamu had been dreading.

"Very interesting, and top marks for initiative and effort. But what has any of this to do with our core business?"

"Frankly, Sir, not a lot," Adamu replied. "Thus far, there isn't anything that suggests top-level police corruption in any of this, but we both feel strongly that a corrupt deal lies at the bottom of the needless deaths of four people, including two toddlers, and we think it's worth pursuing."

"I agree...but not by us. The answer is no." He leaned forward, and started looking through the paperwork on his desk. The meeting was over.

"So, what next?" Bassey asked Adamu somewhat dejectedly, when they were back in the main office.

"Not sure. I'll think of something."

Adamu lay awake in bed later that night turning things over in his mind. Their boss was probably right in forbidding them to continue working on the case–they had, after all, admitted that there wasn't high-level police corruption involved, and that was their job. But it still rankled, and he knew Bassey felt the same way. They had been given a direct order, and neither Adamu nor Bassey was inclined to disobey and face insubordination; that wasn't to say that they had both given up on nailing Big Man. But, how to do so?

Across town from Asokoro, Bassey was also awake in Apo. Because of the time difference between Abuja and Atlanta, he had to stay up late in order to talk with his wife and children on Skype, and seeing his own twins made him doubly determined to bring the killers of Mike's children to book. He had come to admire and respect Mike in the short time he had known him, and Bassey wondered whether he could ever be as strong as Mike had been if anything ever happened to his own family … he shuddered at the thought. He wandered into the kitchen and helped himself to a cold Heineken from the fridge. Opening the bottle with the edge of a spoon, he wandered back into the lounge and slouched on the sofa, propping his feet up on the coffee table. And it was there in that position, about half an hour later, that an idea began to form in his mind.

Adamu must have dozed off, because he woke up with a start when one of his phones went off. Reaching for it, he saw it was one of the numbers that Bassey used. "Do you know what time it is?"

"I think I may have a solution to our problem. I'm on my way. See you in a few." The phone went dead. Bassey rocked up in a few minutes. Adamu looked at him sourly. "This had better be good."

Bassey ignored him and wandered into the kitchen. "Do you have any decent coffee?" he asked, rummaging about in cupboards. Eventually he found some and made coffee. After pouring out coffee for his host, he sat down on a stool with gleaming eyes.

"Well, what's the bright idea then?" Adamu asked. "The boss forbade us from continuing with this investigation, right?"

"Get to the point."

"He didn't say anything, as far as I recall, forbidding Mike from doing so though, did he? And if, every now and then either you or I happen to see or speak with our buddy Mike, and he chooses to bring us up to speed or ask our advice about his investigation, then it would be churlish of us to refuse, wouldn't it?"

"Bassey, you know as well as I do that that's seriously pushing the limits."

"And since when did you turn into such an old woman?"

Adamu suddenly grinned. "Fuck it, let's do it. How do we make it work?"

Abuja, Nigeria, the next morning

Mike stared across the breakfast table at Adamu and Bassey. "What do you mean, I'm going to have to become an undercover cop?"

"Only in a manner of speaking, Sir," Bassey replied soothingly. "The fact is, for reasons we can't really go into, we're going to have to take a back seat on this for a while, so we need you to take up some of the slack, if we're going to nail these bastards. Your friend Akin, as you know, has agreed to work with us, if only to save his own skin. What we need him to do is to manoeuvre Big Man into telling him who else is involved in this Ports concession thing, so we can figure out how we can grab the whole lot of them."

"Guys, you're forgetting the small matter of Big Man's constitutional immunity. He's the bastard behind this, and he's the one I want to nail. So either we remove his immunity by removing him from office, or..." Mike paused as an idea crossed his mind.

"This immunity only exists in Nigeria, right?'

"That's right."

Mike smiled broadly. "We might just have a solution," he announced.

CHAPTER 9

Igore, Nigeria, one week later

AKIN WAS BEGINNING TO WONDER WHETHER HE'D made the right decision after all. He had been expecting to hear from Mike and his friend but the silence had been deafening. It was with great difficulty he had managed to focus in any meaningful way on his duties, but the strain was starting to show. Sade had asked him a few times what the matter was, but the way he had just snapped at her made him ashamed, but there was absolutely no way he could tell her what was going on.

Then his phone rang. "Hello?"

"Akin, this is Mike. Can you come to Abuja in the next few days?"

Akin flipped through his diary. One of the senators from the state was hosting a reception to mark his daughter's wedding in Abuja at the weekend. Akin had originally intended to give it a miss, but it was the perfect excuse for him to be in Abuja at the weekend.

"I can be there on Friday."

"Fine. Give me a call when you get in and we'll take it from there."

Abuja, Nigeria, three days later

Akin was a touch apprehensive as he approached Mike's apartment block. He wasn't sure what exactly to expect, apart from what little Bassey had said at the hotel in Igore, which didn't really amount to much. He looked around the flat after Mike let him in.

"Where's your friend?" he asked with some surprise.

"Not here, clearly. Detained at the office, I gather." Mike really wasn't in the mood for small talk.

"Here's the deal. In the next few days, Big Man, or more accurately, you, will receive, by courier, a package from a law firm in Atlanta called Hill, Ash and Joseph. Inside will be a letter from one of the partners saying that one of their clients, with extensive tobacco and poultry farming interests, is interested in investing in Kauru State, and would like to invite Big Man and a couple of his staff to an initial exploratory meeting in Atlanta; if that goes well, their client would like to send an advance team to do a feasibility study. The key task for you is to persuade him that it's a good idea ... and that you should be on the delegation. Once that's done you'll be briefed on the next stage. Any questions?"

"I don't see —"

Mike cut him off. "No need to see, just do."

When Mike had shown Akin out after confirming contact details, he set to work fleshing out the details of the sting.

Igore, Nigeria, one week later

Akin was surprised how easily persuadable Big Man had been. There had not been any need to push the idea too strenuously, especially as it involved overseas travel at government expense. It also helped to fulfil a campaign promise about attracting investment and creating jobs, which always sounded good in a press release. In fairly short order, the press secretary was summoned and ordered to issue such a release, and the budget director instructed to start working on travel arrangements – Akin had to remind Big Man that they would need to liaise with their US hosts regarding dates.

"Excellency, have you decided who will travel with you?" the chief protocol officer asked.

"Clearly, the commissioners for Trade and Investment and Finance need to be in attendance. Then someone from protocol as well as the ADC," Big Man replied, knowing full well that the chief protocol officer would seize the opportunity to earn herself some estacode in US dollars—and continue the torrid sexual affair she had been having with him over the last few weeks.

"I will draft a reply to the Americans for your signature—or would you rather I replied on your behalf?" Akin asked Big Man.

"Write them back on my behalf, but don't make it sound too eager."

Nnamdi Azikiwe International Airport, Abuja, Nigeria, one month later

Mike and Bassey sat at opposite ends of the departure lounge, waiting to board the Lufthansa flight to Frankfurt. It had been touch and go whether Bassey's somewhat belated request for a month's leave to visit his family in the US would be approved, but in the end, Adamu had swung it by promising their boss that he would be happy to cover for Bassey while he was away. They'd been lucky to get seats on this flight once Akin had confirmed the travel dates of Big Man and his entourage, but it was imperative to the success of Mike's plan that both he and Bassey were in Atlanta for at least a week prior to Big Man's arrival. As it was, Bassey would catch a connecting flight to Atlanta a day ahead of Mike, but that could not be helped. Adamu and Bassey had gone over the plan with Mike again and again, picking it apart and trying to anticipate any and every eventuality. The whole thing was not going to be cheap, but it was worth every penny, Mike thought. He could see Bassey at the other end of the lounge, but as agreed, they kept their distance from each other. Soon, the flight was called and Mike stood up. Game time.

Murtala Muhammed International Airport, Lagos, Nigeria, two weeks later

Big Man settled into his seat in the first class cabin of the British Airways flight to London. He was really looking forward to this trip to the States. It seemed like ages since he had last been, and he missed the place. Besides, there was also the fringe benefit of that saucy protocol officer sitting a few rows behind in business class.

Heathrow Airport, London, England, two days later

Rick Cleland had been very surprised to hear from Mike. They had tried to keep in touch after Mike had left the City Firm all those years ago, but inevitably had drifted apart. He was even more surprised by what Mike had asked of him. He had no idea that the person who was responsible for his trip was sitting several rows ahead of him in seat 2A.

Hartsfield-Jackson International Airport, Atlanta, Georgia

It was not quite the same as sweeping through the airports at home, but there were benefits to travelling on an official passport. Big Man went through Immigration and Customs with no problem, and in fairly short order was being driven into town.

Not far behind, Mike and Bassey had picked up Rick and were also driving into the city. "So, how was the flight?" Mike asked.

"Pretty smooth, actually. Next time, though, do you think you could stretch to a business class seat?" Rick said with a grin, in the Southern drawl that hadn't been modified by several years of living in London, and which was one reason

Mike had enlisted his help in the first place. "What's this all about anyway?"

"We're working together on a major corruption enquiry back home. One of the subjects of that enquiry is in town to meet with some lawyers representing potential investors. You're the partner in charge of this project." Mike passed across a thick envelope to Rick in the back seat of the rented SUV. "There's some homework for you to bone up on tonight. We're going to the office now, so you're familiar with it. Oh, and we'll need to take a photo of you for your office, so I hope you've got some proper clothes with you."

They headed into downtown Atlanta, during which Mike and Bassey gave Rick an edited version of the background to the case and after about 30 minutes Bassey pulled into an underground car park. They took the lift from the car park to the 6th floor and emerged into a foyer with a secretary behind a desk. Bassey smiled at her, turned right and walked down a corridor. He stopped in front of a door with a brass plate on it saying: 'Hill, Ash and Joseph, Attorneys at Law'. He pushed open the door and entered a suite of offices. The outer office was well appointed, but not overdone. There was a receptionist's desk, with the firm's name emblazoned in foot high letters on the wall behind the desk. A few chairs were scattered around the room, with a water cooler in one corner.

Bassey led the way past the reception desk into a corridor with an open-plan office with large glass windows occupying the whole of the right side. On the left were doors with signs such as Library, Conference Room and Registry. A careful observer would have noticed that the computers on the desks in the open plan office were not plugged in, nor were there any books or files in the Library or the Registry. The last door on the left had a sign on it saying Lyndon P. Ash, Managing Partner. Bassey pushed open the door and entered.

"Welcome to your office, Mr Ash," Mike said to Rick.

Rick looked round. "Pretty impressive...does Mr Ash rate his own private bathroom?"

"Behind you and to your right," Bassey replied. "Why?"

"What if my clients want to use the bathroom while they're here?"

Mike turned to Bassey. "See? I told you he was pretty smart for a Yank." Bassey was impressed by the profanity of Rick's response.

Buckhead, Atlanta, later that evening

The three men had just finished a pretty good steak dinner and were still in the restaurant booth nursing brandies. They'd gone over the plan for the next day a few times, and made a few changes. They were fairly content with the final version; even though it wasn't perfect, it would have to do and, they thought, stood a pretty good chance of working.

Bassey raised his brandy glass. "Here's to the success of Operation Laundry."

The other two stared at him. "Why Laundry?"

"Because we're striving to erase a stain on the face of humanity." They clinked their glasses, settled the bill and headed out.

⌘ ⌘

A few miles away, their target was also holding a glass, albeit in somewhat different circumstances. Big Man sprawled on a couch in his suite at the Four Seasons, enjoying the ministrations of his chief protocol officer who was kneeling in front of him. They were both naked. Life doesn't get much better than this, he thought.

Atlanta, Georgia, the next day

Rick was slightly nervous as he awaited the arrival of Big Man and his entourage. He had stayed up late last night after dinner, going through the dossier that Mike had given him the previous day until he was thoroughly familiar with its contents. He had always fancied himself as a bit of an actor — well, here was his chance to prove it, and in a good cause to boot. He was going to be on his own, as Mike and Bassey had decided the previous evening that it would be best if they stayed away from the area entirely to avoid the slightest possibility of being seen. They showed him how to activate the recording device on his desk, and he tested it once or twice until he could do it while ostensibly pressing a buzzer to summon his secretary to bring in refreshments. The secretary, hired by Mike and Bassey from a local bureau, was completely in the dark about the real purpose of the office. So were the two young ladies and three young men who had been hired by Bassey and Mike to dress in business suits and appear to be working in the open plan office — the two hundred dollars apiece they were being paid for a couple of hours pretend work was enough to forestall any questions.

The phone on the receptionist's desk buzzed and she picked it up. "Hill, Ash and Joseph...yes Sir, that's right, we're expecting them. Please send them up." She cut the connection, then pressed a few buttons. The phone on Rick's desk buzzed. "Your guests are on their way up. Shall I bring them in?"

"I'll come meet them myself, thanks." Rick stood up, straightened his tie, and walked to reception. As he passed the open plan office, he tapped on the window and gave the pretend lawyers the thumbs up. They nodded in acknowledgment and started tapping away at lifeless computer keyboards, flipping through files and concentrating on the motley collection of thick books that Mike had purchased a few days before from a used bookstore.

He arrived as the receptionist was ushering Big Man in. "Your Excellency, a pleasure to meet you at last. Lyndon Ash," he said in his most expansive southern drawl, extending a hand to Big Man, who shook it warmly.

"It's good to be here, thank you." He turned and introduced the two commissioners who accompanied him. He did not bother with the protocol officer and the ADC, who retreated to a corner of the reception and sat down as Rick led Big Man and his commissioners along the corridor and into his office, past the hive of activity in the open plan office. He waved his guests in, carefully making sure he sat Big Man down in the place of honour to the right of the desk, closest to the hidden recorder. He sat in his own chair behind the desk.

"Thank you so much again for coming, Sir; my clients also express their gratitude, and hope that we will be able to work together in a mutually beneficial way. But first, can I offer you anything to drink? Tea, coffee, soft drinks, water...or would you prefer something stronger?"

"Coffee is fine for now," Big Man said. His commissioners nodded in agreement.

Rick leaned forward to press the buzzer for the secretary, and at the same time started the recording device.

There was a tap at the door and the secretary entered. "Four coffees, please, with cream and sugar."

"Sure, coming right up," she said and left the office.

Rick noticed that all three of his guests checked her out as she left.

"Gentlemen, my clients are a consortium of businessmen with extensive poultry and tobacco farming interests here in the States as well as in Central and South America. They are now looking to expand into Africa, and have decided that Nigeria would be the obvious choice, given the size of the market and the relative lack of regulation. They are men with contacts and influence, and they advise me that you and your state were recommended to them as the best option to explore. They are also very private individuals, and prefer to go about their business without publicity, and so they have authorised my firm to act for them in this matter, as indeed they have in several other matters, admittedly mostly within the US. In due course, and depending how things proceed, we will seek your recommendations as to the names of reputable legal firms in Nigeria with whom we can engage as corresponding partners." He broke off as the secretary returned with the coffees and a selection of cakes and biscuits, which Rick steered clear of, but which his guests tucked into.

"Sound interesting," Big Man replied, in between mouthfuls of cake. "What exactly do your clients have in mind?"

"They have already commissioned a feasibility study from the point of view of climate, market size, infra- structure requirements, ease of doing business, etc. We understand that this has yielded mixed results—the positive bits being climate and market size, the negative ones being infrastructure and the ease of doing business. They do not regard the latter as being insurmountable, which is where you come in. They will be looking to you to facilitate such things as making land available, assisting with infrastructure development, a favourable tax structure; in return, they will make commitments the regarding creation of local jobs, corporate social responsibility and revenue sharing with the state government."

The finance commissioner spoke for the first time. "And what sort of scale of investment are they talking about here?"

"Two hundred and fifty million US dollars, minimum," Rick replied.

There was silence in the room for a moment as the figure sank in. Eventually Big Man set his coffee cup down and said, "Let's talk business."

"You could almost hear the pinging of the cash registers in their heads as I said that." Rick was sprawled out on the king-size bed in his hotel room as he filled Mike and Bassey in on the day's meeting. "From then on, it was like pushing at an open door. They agreed to most of the conditions I proposed, but pushed back at others; for example, they refused to agree to the consortium having a majority stake in the Nigerian company, and pushed for a greater volume of private shareholdings, but then accepted that the consortium would mainly own the US parent company. It was actually fun, and at times I had to remind myself that the consortium didn't actually exist."

"Excellent, well done Rick, great job," Mike said. Then, as casually as he could manage, "And Big Man agreed to the side issues we discussed?"

"Absolutely. Here." He passed across two pieces of paper with the details of two New York bank accounts. The first one was in the name of a company which would act as the US parent company into which the law firm had ostensibly paid fifty million dollars on behalf of the consortium; the state government would pay ten million dollars into the same account as its own stake in the company. The second piece of paper was the key one — it had details of a US bank account in the joint names of Big Man and his wife, into which, as agreed between Rick and Big Man in a separate conversation without the commissioners being present, four million of the ten million paid by the state government would be diverted, topped up by another million from the consortium. That Big Man had such an account was a clear violation of the Code of Conduct for public officers; the fact that it was being used to launder the proceeds of corruption was a bonus. And it was all caught on tape.

Mike did his best to keep his face impassive. "Great job again, Rick, much appreciated. Of course, none of this ever happened, right?"

Rick grinned broadly. "Do I know you?"

CHAPTER 10

Abuja, Nigeria, ten days later

ADAMU WAS PLAYING HOST TO BASSEY AND MIKE this time as they filled him in on the details of the Atlanta sting. They were all feeling pretty good about how things were progressing. Before leaving Atlanta, Mike and Bassey had first of all made three copies of the tape of the conversations that Rick had had with Big Man and his colleagues, and the one he had with Big Man on his own. They had then painstakingly transcribed the recordings, and Bassey had lodged the originals and a copy each of the tape and transcript in a safety deposit box at his wife's bank in Atlanta; Mike had done the same at his London bank on his way back to Abuja. The third copy had been played for Adamu, and he followed the transcript as he listened. When it was over, he looked up, smiled and nodded. "We've got enough to nail the bastard now."

Bassey nodded. "Maybe, but we still need to get him back to the States without him suspecting that something fishy was going on."

"Well, I may just have the solution to that problem. Remember our murderous friend Morocco?" Adamu asked with a smile.

"What of him?"

"He's had the fear of God truly put into him by our army friends," Adamu replied. "They have him locked up with some suspected Boko Haram insurgents. I have arranged for word to be passed to him that his former employers now know that he is in custody and that they now regard him as an expendable liability—he knows better than most exactly what that means. He is now willing to do anything to save his neck, including setting up his former associates."

Mike frowned. "And how does that help us get Big Man back to the States?"

"Sir, your late wife had dual American and Nigerian nationality, did she not?" Adamu asked.

"That's right, she was born in the States when her parents were doing their postgraduate degrees...and?"

"The Americans take a dim view of their citizens being harmed or killed in the course of terrorist activity. If one of the killers is now in custody as a suspected terrorist, and he implicates others as being responsible for the attack, and if one or more of the said others is found to be laundering the proceeds of corruption in US dollars through a US bank ... getting my drift now, Sir?"

Bassey looked at Adamu with respect. "You really are a devious bastard, you know."

Ibadan, Nigeria, two weeks later

Casablanca was starving. The traffic on the road from Igore had been unusually heavy as the result of an overloaded trailer turning over on its side and partially blocking the road. He'd left home in Igore early that morning after getting a text from one of the aides to the state police commissioner, requesting an urgent out of state meeting with the commissioner in Ibadan that afternoon. Casablanca had thought nothing of the request—he'd had such meetings with the current commissioner and several of his predecessors; doing dirty jobs for politicians was how managed to run his various smuggling rings, protection and political thuggery rackets for so long without much more than token interference from the cops. Still, he had not managed to have breakfast before he left, and although he was running late, he was going to visit his favourite *buka* for a meal of hot *amala and ewedu soup* before the meeting. Besides, the commissioner probably wanted to shake him down for money again — the greed of those bloody policemen was legendary.

Forty minutes later, he emerged from the *buka* feeling pleasantly full. He pulled out his phone to check the address in one of the city's better neighbourhoods where the meeting would take place. He levered himself into the back seat of the SUV, gave directions to his driver, leaned back and shut his eyes for a quick nap before the meeting.

Assistant Superintendent of Police Wale Omojola was an ambitious young man. He quickly realised after he joined the police that the way ahead was to hitch one's wagon to a senior officer who seemed to be heading for the top. With the protection of such a godfather, and a willingness to push the limits, a young man with a bit of sense could go far.

No man's fool, Omojola had taken time to choose, and then ingratiate himself with his godfather, and it would seem he had chosen wisely. The man was now a state police commissioner, and it seemed he was headed for promotion to assistant inspector general. Omojola had sailed merrily along in his boss' wake, learning the ropes of graft and accumulating wealth beyond his income. The future was bright — or at least, so it had seemed before those two gentlemen had paid him a visit at his home a couple of weeks ago. He'd stared dumbfounded as they laid out in cold, unemotional tones the damning evidence of his graft, and then, in even more ominous tones, speculated on the consequences.

Having let him absorb this for a minute, they had then offered him a lifeline. The person they were really after was his boss — if Omojola was prepared to throw him under the bus, they would ensure that he, Omojola, would stay out of jail, and might even get to keep some of his ill-gotten gains. For Omojola, it was a no-brainer, hence the text he sent to Casablanca first thing this morning as instructed, and it explained why he was now in the nondescript bungalow awaiting Casablanca's entry into the trap that Bassey and Adamu had so carefully set. Omojola was aware that some sort of arrest operation was afoot, but not the details. All he knew was that he was to admit Casablanca to the house, and then do as he was told by the same two men, one of whom waited quietly in the room next door, while the other was pretending to be the gate man.

The driver-cum-bodyguard announcing that they had arrived at the address, woke Casablanca. The driver sounded his horn, and Bassey emerged from the gateman's hut.

"Afternoon sah," he greeted the driver.

"Chief Casablanca to see Oga Wale."

"Okay sah," Bassey returned to the gate and opened it. He waved the SUV in, and directed the driver to a carefully chosen spot under the shade of a tree on the right side of the house, from which the view of the front door was partially blocked by a deliberately parked people carrier. Casablanca heaved himself down and walked slowly towards the front door.

Inside, Adamu watched him approach. When Casablanca was a few yards from the door, he nodded at Omojola, who opened the door and smiled broadly at Casablanca. "Welcome Chief, *oga* is inside waiting."

"My brother, how now?" Casablanca responded, shaking Omojola's surprisingly damp hand. Omojola stepped aside and waved Casablanca ahead. He was still idly wondering why the man had not wiped his hands after washing them when he stepped out of the bright afternoon sunshine into the darker and cooler room.

He had taken a few steps into the room before his eyes adjusted to the light—to be confronted by the sight of Adamu smiling at him, with the business end of a large pistol pointing right between his eyes. "Please sit down, and be quiet." Adamu said, jerking his head towards a chair on his left. His eyes, and the pistol's muzzle did not move from a spot right between

Casablanca's eyes. As Casablanca did as he was told, the door opened again, and Bassey and Omojola appeared, pushing the driver in front of them with an equally evil-looking pistol in Bassey's hand a few inches from the driver's right ear. He joined his boss on the couch, Bassey's pistol still inches from his head.

"Cuff them." Adamu instructed Omojola, who did as he was told.

"Pockets," was Adamu's next instruction. Omojola stood each one up in turn, and rapidly emptied their pockets, the contents of which included several wads of cash, while being careful not to get between the pistols and the two captives. Once he was satisfied that their pockets were empty, he made them sit down again. Adamu sat down in front of them, pistol still in hand. Bassey remained standing off to one side, weapon still in hand and pointing at the two men now cuffed on the sofa.

Adamu looked steadily at both men for a minute before speaking. "We have Morocco in custody. He has told us everything about the attack on Mrs Anako and her family in Abuja. We know you were responsible for sending Moroccco and Razor to carry out the operation. That means that you are as guilty as they are. Razor is dead. Morocco has agreed to give evidence against you in order to avoid a death sentence. As things stand right now, you are the only man who is going to hang for this crime." He paused to let that sink in.

Casablanca attempted to bluster. "What do you mean? I don't know anything" — Adamu cut him off. "Shut up and stop wasting your breath, before I take you outside and finish you off just now, and save everyone all the *wahala* of a trial."

Casablanca took the hint and shut up. Adamu continued, "Frankly, it's not really you we're after. Although I think the world would be a far better place without you in it. We know Big Man set this whole thing up. Now, you can either help us to nail him, and in return we'll cut you a deal to avoid the hangman. Or, you can continue to do strong head, and be hanged. Your choice."

Casablanca looked from Adamu to Bassey. Failing to find any shred of sympathy there, he looked to Omojola, who suddenly seemed to find his feet fascinating. He looked back at Adamu and swallowed. "What do you want me to do?"

Lagos, Nigeria, one week later

Alhaji was savouring the cool air from the air conditioner in the living room of his pied-a-tierre in Ikoyi. The three bedroom flat appeared on his company records as an annexe to the head office; in reality, it was the venue for his and his associates' numerous assignations with a variety of women, one of whom he'd just got rid of after a somewhat energetic session. He stretched his legs on the sofa, and took another sip from his beer. It had been an interesting afternoon's diversion, but it was time to get back to the real world. He picked up his phone and called downstairs to his driver to get the car ready.

A few minutes later, he was in the car, heading for the mainland through the Lagos afternoon traffic. Preoccupied with his newspaper, neither he nor his driver took much notice of the grey Volkswagen Passat that was following a few cars behind them. Both cars crawled across the Third Mainland Bridge to Anthony Village. Alhaji's driver turned off into the entrance to the estate he lived in. Again, he failed to notice a nondescript Toyota that was parked just inside the estate behind an SUV with tinted windows. The two men in the front of the Passat swung across the turning to the estate and blocked it, just as the Toyota swung out abruptly and blocked Alhaji's car, which was now neatly boxed in. Too late, Alhaji's driver realised what was going on. Instinctively, he threw the car into reverse, but was blocked by the Passat. Four men in dark clothing with their faces obscured emerged and swung into action. One smashed the driver's window with an iron bar, immediately followed by a second man who reached in and opened the driver's door. As he did so, the first man dropped the iron bar and levelled a pistol at the head of the driver. Simultaneously, the other two men wrenched open the back doors, manhandled Alhaji out, cuffed and gagged him and threw him in the back of the SUV with the dark windows. The whole thing was over in less than a minute, and the attackers were on their way with their prey shortly after.

About an hour later, Alhaji was led from the vehicle. During the journey, his captors had not said a word, but had thrown a bag over his head, so he could now not see as well as not speak. He was helped across some soft ground, and into a building. Still entirely silently, he was guided to a chair, to which he was gently, but securely fastened. A very strong light came on shining directly into his eyes, and the bag over his head removed, blinding him. At the same time, the gag was removed. From somewhere behind the light came a voice with a strong accent.

"Very sorry that you have been brought here like this, Alhaji, but it was very important that you came. I will keep this brief. Your friend, Big Man, his excellency the governor is a criminal, who is deeply implicated in a case of mass murder. We know all about your arrangement on the Ports privatisation matter, and believe me, it would be child's play to rope you in on the murder case as well. Big Man may have immunity, but you do not. In order to avoid that, we need your help to remove his immunity. You will therefore use your extensive connections and huge wealth to buy off the deputy governor and a majority of the Kauru House of Assembly, and arrange for the governor to be impeached — we will provide the evidence for the case against him. If you agree to cooperate, we will say nothing about the murder case against you, and will not bring to light your previous dubious deals with Big

Man. If you do not, one of two things will happen. You will either be shot in the next few minutes and your body dumped in the middle of nowhere, or, after a trial for murder, you will be ignominiously hanged—*after dem don fuck your yansh tire for prison.*" The voice stopped.

Alhaji was still shell-shocked by the ease with which he'd been captured, the circumstances in which he was being held, and the unemotional way in which the faceless voice was discussing his possibly imminent demise. His voice quavered as he attempted to respond. "I, I don't ... I mean, what is going on... ?"

Still very blandly, the voice continued. "Alhaji, I am going to count to ten. If by the time I reach ten, you have not given me an answer, or have said no to my proposal, I will assume that you are tired of life, and will take steps to assist you to depart swiftly, and possibly painfully, from this world. One, two, three..."

"Stop, stop!!" Alhaji shrieked. "I will cooperate, I will do it!"

The voice continued in the same unruffled tone. "I think you have made a wise choice. Shortly, I am going to tell you what exactly you need to do, and when and how you will do it. Before I do so, please let me assure you that if you change your mind, try to double cross us, or try and run to your corrupt police and politician friends, we will know almost before you have done it. Remember how easily we captured you; next time, it will not just be you, but your wives, your eldest son in Baltimore, your daughter in Ilupeju, her two children and your concubine in Sagamu who will all die one by one. Now pay attention."

Igore, Nigeria, four days later

The deputy governor sat in a daze as he looked again in disbelief at the two small pieces of paper in his hands. Fifteen million naira was the amount written on one of the cheques made payable to him; the other, also made payable to him was for fifty million naira. He looked across the table at the man sitting opposite him, whom he had come to know as the governor's principal financial backer; he couldn't quite believe that the same man was willing to spend quite so much money to engineer the removal from office of his protégé. "But, Alhaji, what happened now? What did the governor do to offend you so much? Can we not try to—"

Alhaji cut him off impatiently, thinking what a damn fool the man was. "Are you going to cooperate instead of asking me foolish questions, or do you want to join him out of office?"

As he anticipated, the man's greed got the better of his principles, if indeed he had any. "And you say you will arrange all the evidence and deal with the judges?"

Alhaji opened the case beside him and passed along the lever-arch folder of evidence against Big Man that he had been given by the faceless men who abducted him the week before. "It's all there. I have told a few of the assemblymen that I have left something with you for them, and that they should come and see you … please don't disappoint them. I will tell you when the time is right for you to move."

"Don't worry, Alhaji, you can count on us."

⌘ ⌘

Across town, in the governor's office, Big Man sat oblivious to the trap slowly closing in around him. The next stage in the process was about to begin. A package of documents had arrived from Hill, Ash and Joseph in Atlanta, with a copy of the Articles of Incorporation of the US parent company, showing the state government's 20% stake in that company, and requesting that the state government now remit its agreed payment of $10 million. It also included a formal invitation to Big Man to attend the official launch of the US parent company at the Waldorf Astoria in New York in about four weeks time.

Big Man sat back with a satisfied smile. "I have to say that I'm impressed with these people ... they don't waste time and really put their money where their mouth is."

The finance commissioner nodded, "That's true. Should I table the payment for the next exco meeting?"

"My friend, why are you talking like this? Please call the accountant-general and make sure that payment goes by the end of the week. Don't worry, I will sign a letter authorising you to release the money."

"Sir, are you sure? You know how those people like to make trouble."

"Don't worry, I'm sure." They were words that would come back to haunt him.

Abuja, Nigeria, one week later

Mike had never been in the US Embassy in Abuja before. He looked round with interest as he, Bassey and Adamu sat waiting to be shown into the office of the legal attaché. Things had moved along a fair bit since he had initially conceived this novel approach to bringing the killers of his wife and family to justice. For Mike, the key turning point had been the inspired use of Omojola to lure Casablanca into the trap; this had not only provided direct evidence of Big Man's complicity in the murders of Mike's family and his driver, it had also provided usable evidence of big time corruption by Omojola's boss, the commissioner of police, which had enabled Adamu and Bassey to persuade their boss to change his mind and officially sanction their involvement in the investigation. This in turn meant that they could tap into official resources to do things like lift and suborn Alhaji, and ensure the safe and official incarceration of Casablanca and Morocco. It also gave them the authority to arrange the meeting they were about to hold.

The door opened, and the legal attaché came out. "Gentlemen, I'm so sorry to have kept you waiting ... I was on a teleconference with the States that went on forever." As light woman of mixed-race origins, she looked more like a primary school teacher than the seasoned law enforcement agent she was. She extended her hand and shook all three men in turn. "Sara Richardson. Please come in."

They sat around a small conference table. "Can I offer you guys a drink? Water, soft drinks, coffee?. . . Uncle Sam doesn't stretch to booze during working hours, sadly – some days in this place you could really murder a cold beer," she said with a smile.

"Water's fine for me," Mike replied; the other two nodded in agreement.

Niceties done, they got down to business. "So guys, how can the United States be of assistance?" Sara asked. "How about a multiple murder, including of an American citizen in the course of laundering the proceeds of a corrupt business deal, in US dollars, through a US bank?" Bassey replied.

Sara smiled. "You really know how to get a girl's attention, don't you?"

Three hours later, Sara showed the men out of her office. "Gentlemen, thanks so much. As I said, I'll need to think about this and consult Washington. I'll give you a ring in a couple of days with an update." Returning to her office, she sat down and looked through her notes of the meeting. She reflected for a bit, then reached forward and pressed a few buttons on her phone. "Fred, can I come up in a few? I'm sitting on something here I think the boss needs to know about."

U.S. Attorney's Office, Manhattan, New York, two weeks later

The conference room was a little crowded. In addition to the US Attorney himself, there were representatives from the FBI, the State Department, the New York Police Department, the Justice Department and US Immigration.

Patrick O'Malley was a hard boiled prosecutor, whose many detractors accused him of almost messianic zeal in his enthusiasm for going after wrongdoers of all stripes; he wore this criticism almost as a badge of honour—in his book, criminals belonged in jail and not on the streets. Unfortunately for Big Man, Mr O'Malley reserved his most virulent hatred for those who killed children, smuggled drugs, sex offenders or corruptly betrayed the trust of the public—it seemed to him that his intended quarry ticked at least two of those boxes although, sadly, he would only be able to pursue him on one of them.

"Ladies and gentlemen, if you'll take your seats we'll make a start. Thank you all for coming to this meeting. Before I get into the briefing, can I please emphasize to all present that what I am about to tell you will be held tightly and will not, under any circumstances, go beyond this room. As some of you will be aware, the subject of our meeting today is the man whose face you see on the screen. His name is Domfas Alli, more popularly known as 'Big Man', and he is currently the governor of a state called Kauru in Nigeria. We have credible information that in the process of trying to conclude a corrupt deal, he arranged for a gun attack on the wife and family of an official he perceived as an obstacle to the deal, resulting in the deaths of four people, including two minors. At least one of those people, the wife of the official, was an American citizen; it is possible that the minors were too, although that is currently being clarified. We also have pretty clear evidence that this individual has violated the laws of his country and of the US by maintaining a bank account here in the New York, and using that account to launder the proceeds of corrupt kickbacks from a proposed farming project. I am not worried about the former, but I certainly am about the latter. In addition, depending on the availability of the key witnesses, it may well be possible to prosecute him in a US court for the murder of at least one, maybe more, US citizens abroad. In the meantime, I intend to prosecute him on racketeering and money laundering charges." He paused and looked around the table. He had everybody's undivided attention.

"The thought may well have occurred to you to wonder where this man is. The answer is, in Nigeria right now. But, he is scheduled to arrive in New York in just over a week, which is when we will make our move. Given the international nature of this case, and the suspect's official position, we required the involvement of the State Department. Mr Kaminski here represents the State Department." O'Malley nodded to a tall, grey-haired man with rimless glasses seated to his left.

Kaminski cleared his throat, shuffled the papers in a folder in front of him, and tried to look important, an attempt ruined by his surprisingly high-pitched voice. "The suspect in this case is, as you have heard, a state governor. He is likely, as most senior government officials in Nigeria do, to be travelling on an official, or even a diplomatic passport. We are able to confirm that neither document can, in theory, prevent his being arrested, detained or tried, since the first does not provide immunity at all, and the second only provides immunity to the country to which the holder is accredited as a diplomat, which does not apply in this case. Having said that, arresting this individual is likely to provoke a diplomatic uproar, although both the US Embassy in Nigeria and the State Department in Washington have given the go-ahead."

Mr Kaminski's tone and manner made it abundantly clear how little he thought of that decision. "I have been asked to remain close to the investigation and provide advice on the diplomatic front as required or necessary." Mr Kaminski clearly thought even less of that task.

"Thank you, Sir," O'Malley said crisply. "As you are aware, this case will be prosecuted by the federal government, under federal law and in federal court. Nevertheless, we will need to work in partnership with our colleagues in the NYPD. Assistant Special Agent in Charge Holmes of the FBI and Assistant Chief Collins of the NYPD are both here to brief us. Gentlemen?"

Collins of the NYPD, a stocky, barrel-chested man with closely cropped grey hair spoke first. "This is clearly a federal show, so we're happy to let Jim here and his feds take the lead and do the actual take-down. Happy to provide transport and other backup as required, most likely security in and around court and during transit to and from court."

Holmes of the FBI spoke next. Assistant Special Agent-in-Charge Holmes was not your archetypal clean cut FBI agent — the top button on his shirt was undone, his tie slightly askew and both his hair and bushy moustache could have done with a trim. He looked like the manager of a hardware store — several involuntary guests of the United States Government, now sewing mailbags in federal prisons could testify to the folly of underestimating Agent Holmes.

"Thanks Ben, much appreciated. I'm going to suggest we make the actual arrest away from the airport. I understand the suspect is booked in at the Waldorf. I propose to do the takedown in his hotel room, and then remove him via a service elevator into a car waiting in the basement. May I suggest that we aim for an early arraignment? That way, we can get him safely remanded in custody, which is what I presume you'll be asking for? Flight risk and all that?"

O'Malley nodded. The trap was beginning to close.

CHAPTER 11

Lagos, Nigeria, one week later

BIG MAN SAT BACK IN HIS OFFICIAL CAR AND STARED idly out of the window as the lights of Lagos at night flashed past his window. He was being driven to the airport to catch his flight to New York, accompanied by the usual flashing lights and sirens of his convoy. He had been looking forward to this trip, both as a short break from the daily grind of being governor and because of what the trip represented—a useful and welcome addition to his retirement fund. Ordinarily, he would by now be contemplating what entertaining distractions would be on the agenda, but for some reason, he felt a vague sense of foreboding he couldn't get rid of.

New York, two hours later on the same day

Assistant Special Agent in Charge Jim Holmes was in the room that had been turned into the operations centre at the FBI New York Office in the Jacob Javits Federal Office Building in Manhattan. Sitting around the table listening to the briefing that Holmes was delivering were the ten or so men and women that would be responsible for Operation Little Boy, as some office wag had dubbed the arrest and prosecution of Big Man. Apart from the FBI itself, there were representatives from the NYPD and the USA attorney's office. Holmes was just finishing his briefing when there was a tap at the door and one of his agents entered and handed him a piece of paper. Holmes read for a minute then looked up with a smile. "Ladies and gentlemen, we have just received confirmation that the Delta flight from Lagos to New York has just cleared Nigerian airspace — with our friend safely seated in seat 1A in First Class."

Lagos, Nigeria, the following day

The call Alhaji had been expecting came around 7 a.m. As usual, the number was withheld, but the voice was the same chilling, unemotional and strongly accented one that had so terrified him that terrible night a few weeks ago — and had continued to do so ever since.

"Alhaji?"
"Yes, it's me."
"Time to put our agreement into motion."
"I will do so straight away."
"Good." The line went dead.

Igore, Nigeria, ten minutes later

The deputy governor was still in bed when his phone rang. He saw that it was Alhaji. "Hello Sir, good morning."

"Good morning to you too. Please put the plan into action today."

"No problem, Alhaji."

⌘ ⌘

The news broke at lunchtime. The Kauru State House of Assembly had, seemingly out of the blue, moved a motion of impeachment against Big Man. A large majority passed the motion, accompanied by an extensive dossier detailing several allegations of corrupt practices including contract awards bypassing due process, bribery and nepotism. Accordingly, the House had sent a letter to the State Chief Judge asking him to convene a panel to investigate the allegations and report back to the House within seven days. By the evening news bulletins, the names of the investigation panel members had been published, and a letter sent to Big Man's office informing him of the charges and inviting him to respond to them.

Manhattan, New York

Big Man was shopping on 5th Avenue. He hadn't been able to shake the feeling of unease that he had on his way to the airport in Lagos, and had subsequently not been able to sleep as well as he usually did on long haul overnight flight. At least he did not have to wait too long to clear immigration and customs at JFK, and he'd been ensconced in his suite at the Waldorf in fairly quick time. Whatever was on his mind seemed to have abated, as he downed a couple of brandies before hitting the sack, and he actually slept quite well. After a leisurely breakfast, he decided to browse the shops. His new protocol officer came up to him and handed him one of his phones, which was buzzing. The old one had had to go—she'd started to get a bit too big for her boots just because he screwed her a few times. Glancing down, he saw that it was Akin.

"Hello?"

"Excellency, it's Akin. You need to get back here o, and quickly. *Alarm don blow o!*"

"Calm down and stop panicking. What's happening?"

The FBI agent who'd been tailing him since he left the hotel would later tell her fellow agents it was the first time she had ever seen a black man go pale. She watched as he spoke on the phone, his eyes first widening, and then narrowing. Abruptly he terminated the call and headed for the exit, his companions scurrying to keep up with him. The agent spoke softly into the discreet microphone concealed in the brooch on her lapel. "Subject exiting the store on to 5th. He seems in a hurry."

Her colleague outside the store who to all intents and purposes seemed to be a tourist standing on the sidewalk peering at a map of the city picked up the message and Big Man simultaneously.

He murmured into his microphone. "Subject in view, walking briskly towards the Waldorf. I'm following."

Big Man was strangely relieved. At least he now knew why he had had the feeling of something not being quite right. Those ungrateful bastards in the House of Assembly did not know with whom they were messing. He wasn't called Big Man for nothing. Whatever they have been paid by whoever had put them up to this, he would double it—the reckoning could come later. Right now, he needed to get back. As he swept into his suite, he barked instructions over his shoulder to his staff. "Get on the phone to Delta and all the other airlines and book us on the next flight to Lagos." They jumped to obey.

Igore, Nigeria, the same day

Akin cut the connection to Big Man and put down the phone. He stared down at the letter from the assembly on his desk. Suddenly the bile rose in his throat and he barely made it to the bathroom before throwing up.

Abuja, Nigeria, the same day

Mike looked at his companions, wondering what Bassey and Adamu were thinking. They were sitting in Adamu's flat, staring at the phones on the table in front of them, willing one of them to ring. The tension was thick enough to cut with a knife. In a corner, the TV was tuned in to a local station with the volume turned down. A banner ran across the bottom of the screen announcing over and over again the **breaking news** that 'Assembly serves impeachment allegations to Kauru Gov'. It all seemed to be going smoothly, but the final piece in the jigsaw was still to fall in place.

Manhattan, New York, later that day

Jim Holmes stuck his head round the door of the Ops Centre. A map of the city was projected onto a screen, with the Waldorf and JFK Airport highlighted. A large desk occupied the middle of the room with several chairs arranged around it, and two or three telephones, a couple of radio handsets and one or two computers on it. Off to one side, a couple of agents sat peering at monitors with headphones clamped on their heads. "Any news?"

The shift leader replied. "No Sir, not yet. We know they've got two seats on the Lufthansa flight tonight to Frankfurt and are still waiting for confirmation of the onward connection to Nigeria."

"Let me know as soon as you hear anything."

"Yes Sir."

Holmes wasn't happy with making the arrest outside the hotel, but the flight situation, and the hotel's squeamishness about something as distasteful as an arrest on their premises had conspired against his original plan to arrest Big Man in his hotel room. He would accordingly be a little antsy until the subject was safely arrested and in custody.

A few minutes later, one of the other agents with the headphones on turned and spoke to the shift leader. "Seems they've confirmed their flights. They're rolling." The shift leader nodded an acknowledgement, picked up the phone in front of him and pushed a few buttons. "Sir, looks like they're moving."

Holmes was back in the room in seconds. "Alert the arrest team, and make sure the surveillance teams have eyes on throughout," he barked to the shift leader.

The young agent thought the Old Man was starting to lose the plot a bit—this was a corrupt tin-pot politician they were after, for crying out loud, not a dangerous foreign intelligence agent or drug cartel hit man. Still, orders were orders, so he nodded dutifully, picked up a radio handset and passed on the orders.

A few blocks away, Big Man sat in the back of the hired

limousine, lost in thought. He was perplexed as to how his usually sensitive antennae had picked up no sign of the plot against him—that there was a plot he was not in any doubt about. He wondered who was really behind it, but what little information he'd been able to get from home suggested that a majority of those bastards in the House of Assembly, the state chief judge, and even perhaps his own deputy governor were in on it. Well, he thought grimly, they would all rue the day they allowed themselves to be bought like so many whores in a brothel. But first, he had to catch that flight, and Manhattan traffic wasn't playing ball. Where was a Nigerian Mobile Police escort when you needed one?

JFK Airport, New York, one hour later

Big Man was in a hurry. His protocol officer went to sort out the check-in formalities with the airline, but was back in a few seconds. "Sir, they say they need to see you before they can check you in."

Big Man's temper was in danger of boiling over. Forcing himself to stay calm, he made his way to the first class check in desk.

"Hello Sir, how are you?" the middle-aged woman behind the desk said with a smile.

"Fine," came the somewhat irritable response.

"What is your final destination today?"

"Abuja. Can we get on with it? I'm in a hurry."

"Sure ... do you prefer an aisle or a window seat?"

"I really don't care."

"Okay, Sir, no problem." She tapped away at her keyboard, then asked "Are you checking any bags?"

"No."

"Travelling light, huh? Love it!" Big Man wished she would shut up and let him get the hell out here and go deal with the situation at home.

Finally, she handed over a couple of boarding passes and his passport. "You're all set. Your departure gate is B16, and the lounge is beside Gate B12. You need to clear security first, of course, so turn left at the end of the row of desks and follow the signs. Have a great flight!"

Big Man took the documents from her, didn't bother to respond to her good wishes and turned away, handing the documents to his protocol as he did so. He headed towards security.

"Sir, Special Agent Petrocelli, FBI. Can we have a word? Please step this way."

Abuja, Nigeria, early hours of the following day

The ringing of the phone sounded surprisingly loud in the stillness of Adamu's flat. All three of them stared at the instrument for a few seconds, then, with studied casualness, Adamu picked it up.

"Hello? Yes. That's right, yes. Okay, thank you very much." Still with the same studied casualness, he replaced the phone on the table.

"Well?" Bassey said, trying to match Adamu's casualness and failing miserably.

Adamu stood up. "Congratulations, gentlemen, the first phase is over. Big Man was arrested at JFK about an hour ago. He is now in FBI custody and will appear in court tomorrow."

Mike exhaled deeply. He had not realised he'd been holding his breath. "Well, seems like the Big Apple beckons."

Bassey was on his way to the kitchen. "Never mind about apples, where's the brandy?"

⌘ ⌘

Later that afternoon, slightly the worse for wear, Adamu and Bassey drove with Mike to a smart looking apartment complex in the Wuse area of Abuja. Beyond saying that their boss wanted to meet with him, they were both noncommittal about what the meeting was about. They had all stayed up till almost dawn, savouring Big Man's arrest and talking about the next steps in the case. After getting the nod from Sara Richardson at the US Embassy, a few discreet phone calls had ensured that news of the arrest was the lead item on several TV and radio news programmes in the morning. Not that they'd seen or heard much of the programmes—they crashed, tired, happy and a little drunk just after 7 a.m. They finally got themselves up around lunchtime, Mike and Bassey returning to their own homes to shower and freshen up.

They found somewhere to park and took the stairs to the second floor. Bassey knocked on the door of one of the flats, and a diminutive man dressed very simply in matching tunic and trousers opened the door. Mike was slightly startled to hear Bassey and Adamu greet him with a respectful, "Good afternoon, Sir." He had half expected the man to be a steward or some such person.

"Come on in," he said, turning and leading the way into the flat. He waved them to the chairs in the sitting room. "Grab a seat, I won't be a minute," he said, carrying on into a corridor beyond the sitting room. Mike sat down, looking around as he did at the sparsely but tastefully furnished room. Along one wall was a set of bookcases with several interesting looking volumes. On the walls hung a few oil paintings depicting rural Nigerian scenes. Mike was struck by the absence of any photographs in the room. He turned to his companions just as their host came back into the room.

"So this is the Mr Anako I've been hearing so much about," he said with a slight smile.

"Sir, you have the advantage, Bassey and Adamu have said virtually nothing about you, Mr . . ."

His host smiled. "James Aloysius. These two characters work with me, after a fashion."

"A pleasure to meet you Sir, and thank you for letting them help with my attempt to bring our friend in New York to justice."

"I'm glad you brought that up. We need to think through how we move forward from this point. You can be sure that our friend will mobilise heaven and earth to fight the charges against him, and a satisfactory outcome, from our point of view at least, is by no means guaranteed. But, first, shall we have some lunch? All three of you look as if you could do with some sustenance after a long night drinking."

Abuja, Nigeria, two days later

The conference room at the US Embassy was significantly bigger than the legal attaché's office that they had first met in. It was also more crowded – in addition to Sara Richardson, there were a number of other staffers from the embassy present, as well as officials from the Federal Ministry of Justice in Abuja. Mike took a back seat and left the talking to Adamu and Bassey. He looked curiously around the room and tried to work out exactly what everyone in the room truly did – he noticed that a few people had been introduced or had introduced themselves only by either their first or last names only, and not using both. In between paying attention to the dry legal discussion going on around the table about the laws regarding the prosecution of offenders in a jurisdiction different from the one in which at least some of the alleged offences had been committed, his mind kept returning to the meeting a couple of days earlier with James Aloysius, Adamu and Bassey's boss. Mr Aloysius had, in a dry and understated way, made it clear to Mike, and to his subordinates, that their job was far from over. He had set out all the hurdles that still needed to be overcome if Big Man was to be held accountable for his crimes, some of which were being repeated around the table. Big Man had the financial clout to retain the services of one of America's top lawyers, who would use every legal trick in the book—jurisdiction and procedural matters, not to talk of razor-sharp courtroom skills—to try and get their client off the hook. One of the things that Mr Aloysius had said, and which had thus far not been said in this meeting, was that Big Man still had loyalists within the system in Nigeria, who would do their best to undermine the officially-stated government policy of full cooperation with the US authorities. A trial, never mind a conviction and custodial sentence, was far from a done deal.

Mike had been impressed and reassured by Mr Aloysius's plan to use him as an informal back channel through which he would funnel required information to the US authorities and vice-versa. In the same dry way, he had suggested to Mike that he would have to accept that taking on this role would involve some degree of risk of harm to himself, and that in the circumstances, it would be prudent if he relocated outside Nigeria for at least the duration of the legal proceedings, which would take several months at least. Mike was booked to fly out of the airport in Abuja that evening, ostensibly for a short vacation in Dubai, from where he would eventually make his way to the US via Europe.

Mike returned his attention to the meeting, which appeared to be folding up. Sara Richardson was speaking. "Ladies and gentlemen, thank you all for coming. I hope you'll agree with me that this was a productive meeting and that we've cleared up a number of issues. I'm sure this spirit of cooperation between our two countries will continue as it has always done. We will convene again in about six weeks or so, depending on the progress of proceedings in New York. Thanks again, and enjoy the rest of the day."

The scraping sound of chairs being pushed back filled the room as people stood up. Bassey came over to Mike. "That wasn't too bad, considering nobody sitting around that table really meant a single word they said. Never mind, it's been seen to be done. Ready to go?"

"Yep. Not sure though why I need you guys as nursemaids to get me to the airport, considering that I've been travelling on my own since the age of nine."

Bassey shook his head sorrowfully. "You know, Sir, for someone so bright you can be so not with it sometimes. These people will stop at nothing if they think it'll help their cause, as the attack on your family showed."

Mike nodded ruefully. "Point taken."

Adamu finished off his conversation with Sara Richardson and joined them. "We good to go?"

"Lead on, dear boy, lead on" Bassey replied with a mock flourish.

"Idiot."

CHAPTER 12

JFK Airport, New York, one week later

MIKE WAS GLAD TO STEP OFF THE EMIRATES AIRLINE flight from Dubai. True, there were worse ways of making a long-haul flight than in the business class cabin of an Airbus A380, but it was still 13 hours cooped up in a large metal tube, and it was nice to have his feet on solid ground again. He hadn't realised just how physically and mentally draining the events of the last few weeks had been until he'd had the opportunity, far from the stress of Nigeria, to unwind in Dubai, although that in itself held bittersweet memories of the time that he and Ronke had spent there on their honeymoon. He slept a lot, got back into his exercise regime with a vengeance, and indulged himself once or twice with excellent meals and some superb wines. He even managed to visit a couple of the other emirates that he had not previously been to, in between checking in with James Aloysius in Nigeria as agreed. All in all, he felt a darned sight better than he had in a long time.

He stood in line at immigration, endured the usual biometric data capture stuff, retrieved his bags and cleared customs in, by American standards, fairly short order. He even managed to get a taxi driven by a driver not inclined to make small talk, which was fine by Mike, and was soon on his way to his hotel in mid-Manhattan. The room wasn't great, but it was functional, and would do. Mike unpacked and had a shower. Checking his watch, he saw he still had a couple of hours to kill before making the prearranged call to the number that Mr Aloysius had given him which he had memorized. He slipped into a pair of jeans and a shirt, and went in search of one of the several Chinese buffet restaurants he had spotted on the drive to the hotel. He rejected several before settling for one that did not seem to guarantee, as the others appeared to, death in fairly rapid order from food poisoning. The food, to his surprise, actually did not taste bad at all, and he washed it down with a couple of bottles of Chinese beer. Settling his bill, he made his way back to his hotel room. Checking his watch, he saw that he still had a few minutes before the appointed time. Eventually, the time ticked round, and he dialled the number he had been given. The phone rang a few times, and then a lady's voice answered. "Hi, thanks for calling Larry's Perfumes, how can I assist you today?"Mike was slightly taken aback—for some illogical reason, he had not expected to hear a woman's voice. He quickly gathered his wits. "Hi, I was calling to ask if you stock a men's fragrance called Xerxes?"

"Hold on, one second, I'll ask my manager." She was back in less than 10 seconds. "Yes Sir, we do, but don't have any right now. We are expecting some in a stock delivery tomorrow. If you call between 11 a.m. and noon tomorrow, we should be able to confirm. Or you could stop by if you're in the area, the address is 1880 West 45th Street."

"1880 West 45th Street, right?" Mike repeated. "That's right Sir."

"Thanks very much. I'll be there just after 11."

"Sure thing. Have a good day". The line went dead.

Mike replaced the phone and repeated the address several times to make sure he had committed it to memory. Suddenly feeling tired and sleepy, he undressed, got into bed, and, still repeating the address in his head, drifted off to sleep.

New York, the next day

Mike stepped out of the taxi at the 1600 block of East 42nd street. He was heading for 1780 East 42nd Street, having, as per his instructions from Mr Aloysius, amended the address he had been given yesterday by going East, rather than West, and deducting 100 from the block number and 3 from the street number. Mike thought it was all a bit melodramatic, but he was playing with spooks now and had to follow their rules. 1780 East 42nd Street was another high-rise building that seemed to be what Manhattan consisted entirely of. He approached the entrance and scanned the large buzzer panel on the right-hand side. Quickly locating the one he wanted, he pressed the button next to it. The same woman he had spoken to the day before answered. "Larry's Perfumes."

"Hi, I rang yesterday regarding a men's fragrance called Xerxes which you said you'd have in stock today."

"Sure. Come in and take the elevator to the 26th floor. I'll be waiting." A buzzer sounded and Mike pushed the door open. As instructed, he crossed the lobby in the direction of the sign for the lifts. Unusually, the lobby was entirely deserted, but Mike felt, in a strange way, that he was being watched. Entering the lift, he pressed the button for floor 26. Emerging from the lift, he was met by a tall, middle-aged woman with blonde hair generously flecked with grey. She smiled at him. "Hi, you must be Mike. Please follow me." She turned and walked to Mike's right, passing several doors with no signs on them. Stopping at one that was indistinguishable from the several other ones they'd walked past, she turned to him, and in a slightly apologetic tone said, "I'm afraid you'll have to empty your pockets and be screened when we get in — standard procedure for all visitors." She pressed the badge she was wearing on a lanyard around her neck against a panel at the side of the door and a green light came on. Pushing the door open, she entered and beckoned Mike in. He stepped into an anteroom that had a bank of CCTV screens against one wall, opposite which was a desk, behind which sat a couple of men observing both the screens and Mike. He could see that the screens covered the approaches to the building, front and rear, the entrance, the lobby and the corridor they'd just walked down—that explained his feeling of being watched in the lobby. Directly in front of him was an airport-style magnetometer. His escort walked through it, then handed Mike a small basket round the side of it. Mike dutifully emptied his pockets into it, adding his watch and belt at her request. One of the men behind the desk came to Mike, relieving him of the basket, and also of his shoes, which he passed through a scanner off to one side that Mike hadn't spotted. He walked through the magnetometer when his female escort indicated that he should do so. The man who had passed his belongings through the scanner now approached him.

"Sir, I need to give you a quick pat-down search. Could you please stand with your legs slightly apart, and hold your arms out for me, please?"

Mike did as he was told, noting that as the first man expertly frisked him, he never got between Mike and the second man, whose eyes never left Mike's. Satisfied, the first man returned Mike's belongings with a smile and a polite "Thank you so much for your cooperation, Sir."

Retrieving his belongings, Mike slipped his shoes back on and replaced his belt and the contents of his pockets. His female escort waited till he was done and then said "This way Sir." She was standing by the desk. Mike looked puzzled, and was about to open his mouth to say something when a section of the wall behind the desk slid aside with a hydraulic hiss. Waving him through into what seemed like another small corridor, she stepped in after him, and the wall slid shut behind her. A couple of seconds later, a section of the far wall slid open with the same noise and she waved him through.

"Good morning, Mr Anako, my name is Patrick O'Malley, and I'm the US Attorney in New York. This is Special Agent Holmes of the FBI. We're really glad that you were able to come and help us out with this case. Please grab a seat. I hope you weren't too put out by our security precautions. Unfortunately, bitter experience has taught us that it's better to be safe than sorry when dealing with the bad guys. Coffee?"

U.S. Attorney Patrick O'Malley was a tall man, well over six feet, with the muscular physique of the football player he'd been at Boston College in his youth. Now in his mid-forties, his reddish hair was greying at the temples, and was starting to thin at the top. Many a witness had wilted in court under the icy glare of his blue-grey eyes.

Mike shook hands with both men and sat down. "Thanks, a black coffee would be great. Mr Aloysius did warn me that it would be like this."

Holmes turned from the coffee pot and spoke for the first time as he handed the coffee cup to Mike. "How is James? I haven't seen him for a while. A very canny operator, that man — shame your country's law enforcement community doesn't have more professionals like him."

"I don't really know him that well. I only ever met him once. I'm more familiar with a couple of his subordinates. As you probably know, I'm not a cop — just a lawyer turned investment banker." Mike accepted the coffee and took a sip.

"Yes, we are aware of that. Your friends Adamu and Bassey will eventually show up and will be the official liaison people between the Nigerian authorities and us. James, wily old fox that he is, is determined to take no chances with this case, and came up with using you as a back-channel to pass information between us to avoid the risk of compromising information, by passing it through official channels." Holmes replied.

"So, what exactly do you need me to do?" Mike asked.

Metropolitan Correction Center, Manhattan, New York
One week later

Big Man was dressed in an ill-fitting prison-issue orange

jumpsuit, looking slightly haggard. He stared across the table at his lawyer. The man had to be joking. "What did you just say?"

J. Henry Winthrop IV, dressed in an expensive Italian silk suit, and looking smug and well-fed, stared right back. He wasn't used to visiting his clients in the less than salubrious circumstances he found himself in currently, but that did not mean he was about to be intimidated by Big Man. After all, as his name implied, he came from a long line of distinguished, exclusive, expensive and wealthy lawyers, and Big Man wasn't the first state governor that he had represented.

"You heard me. The judge has denied our motion for bail on the basis that the court regards you as a flight risk. That cute bastard O'Malley swung it by also lodging an application for a Grand Jury indictment for 'being an accessory to murder', which I bet he will now not push for, although leaving it on file. In any event, as I think I told you, bail was always a long shot. We need to now start formulating trial strategy, so I suggest we focus on that."

"Are you seriously telling me that I'm going to stay in this shit hole till the trial? And when is that likely to be?"

"We're pushing for an early date — with luck, we'll be on in about six weeks, if O'Malley keeps his word."

"So what the hell am I paying you all that money for?"

"To make sure you're here for the shortest possible time — six weeks here as opposed to 60 years somewhere less pleasant. Now, can we make a start?"

United States District Court for the Southern District of New York, six weeks later

The atmosphere was reminiscent of a Hollywood film premiere. Across the road from the court entrance, a profusion of TV cameras, satellite vans and long lens press cameras bristled. A number of groups, either supporting or against

Big Man, waved placards and chanted slogans at each other over the heads of the lines of police that kept them apart. The waiting press pack shouted questions across the road as various important-looking people scurried into the building, but they really got excited when Big Man's lawyer stepped out of a gleaming black limousine and swept across the street towards the waiting pack of journalists, trailing a posse of file-carrying minions in his wake. Ignoring the frenzy of questions, he paused for a second to slick down his hair and straighten his tie before lifting both hands for silence.

"Ladies and gentlemen, we will be going to trial shortly in a case that represents, in our view, one of the most flagrant abuses of government power that I have ever seen in my twenty-five years of trying cases. We will conclusively show that the government has no case against my client, and, after, as we anticipate, the court throws out these preposterous charges, we will be seeking serious reparation for our client from the government. Thank you very much." And with that, he turned on his heel and walked in to the courthouse.

A few minutes later, he swept into the courtroom, nodding curtly to the prosecution table as he did so. A few minutes later, the US marshals brought in Big Man. Six weeks in custody had resulted in a somewhat trimmer Big Man, who looked even sharper than usual in his tailored suit. He waved at his family sitting on the public benches, and then sat down with his lawyer.

"So, how's it looking?" he said as he leant across to Winthrop.

The lawyer paused for a moment as he considered his response. His client, like every politician he had ever defended, was someone he held in some contempt, partly because so many of them were the *nouveau-riche* type he detested, and partly because the size of their egos offended the narcissist in him. Still, the man was paying his not inconsiderable fees, so he had to be humored — the holiday home in the Bahamas, the ski lodge in Colorado and the yacht moored in the Florida keys had to be paid for somehow, after all.

"The first step is challenging the court's jurisdiction to try you on these charges; we may get lucky on that, but I doubt it. Next, jury selection. As I explained before, we'll be aiming to keep the numbers of white people and women on the jury down — those are two demographics that aren't favourable to you, given the nature of the case and the personalities involved. Once that's done, we'll attack every single strand of evidence the government brings forward on admissibility grounds. We'll see where we are after the government rests."

"Okay, fine. Just get me out of this damn place."

Newark Liberty International Airport, New Jersey, four days later

Mike smiled at the car rental attendant as she handed him the keys and directed him to where the car was parked in the lot. He located the mid-size Toyota without much difficulty. Settling into the car, he found the GPS satellite navigation device and plugged it in. Once it had powered up, he entered the address he had been given by Special Agent Holmes. The satellite navigation device directed him out of the parking lot towards the city. About forty minutes later, it announced that he had reached his destination, which turned out to be a small restaurant called Dusty's, which announced itself as the home of the hickory smoked rib. As instructed, he entered and said he was there joining the Smith party of four. He was directed to a booth at the far end of the restaurant.

"Evening Sir, how are you? Nice to see you again."

Somehow, Mike was not surprised to see Bassey grinning broadly at him, with a beer in front of him. Opposite him sat Special Agent Holmes, who managed to look menacing despite being dressed in jeans and a casual button-down shirt. Mike slid in next to Bassey and was about to ask where Adamu was when that worthy approached the booth from the direction in which Mike had noticed the washrooms were signposted.

"Evening all, looks like you guys have started without me," Mike said. "Any chance a man could get a glass of beer from that pitcher, or are you planning to drink it all yourselves?"

"No problem Sir." Bassey poured Mike a glass as Adamu sat down.

"When did you two characters get into town?" Mike asked.

"I came in a couple of days ago, Sir, but Bassey only got in yesterday," Adamu replied.

"And very helpful they've been too," Holmes added. "O'Malley's generally pleased with how jury selection went, although he would have preferred another couple of white women being empanelled. More importantly, the judge knows Winthrop well, and saw right through all the jurisdictional challenge bullshit he tried to run past her. The real work starts tomorrow with the opening addresses. But, first, shall we order some of the excellent ribs they serve here?"

Once they had eaten, Holmes set out in some detail the lines of attack that the prosecution intended to take against Big Man, with the other three chiming in with suggestions for Holmes to pass on to O'Malley to consider. Holmes also explained how he and his team thought Winthrop and his team would attack the prosecution evidence. There was, apparently, some divergence of opinion in the US Attorney's Office as to whether to base the case mainly on documents or on witnesses. While the authenticity of documents could be challenged, they had the supreme advantage of being impossible to cross-examine. Plus, the core of the money laundering case rested on documents that had been produced by US institutions. A case resting solely on documents did not have the newsworthiness of witnesses making dramatic revelations on the stand, which appealed to the show man in O'Malley; witnesses, however, were apt to be confused, and trapped into contradicting themselves in the hands of a skilled cross-examiner, which Winthrop undoubtedly was. And, they also ran the risk of rubbing the jury up the wrong way. Holmes, ever the hard-headed pragmatist, was less interested in headlines and more interested in getting a conviction, a viewpoint shared by the other three; Adamu and Bassey because they were cut from the same law enforcement cloth as Holmes, and Mike because, more than anything else in his life, wanted to see the man responsible for the death of his family behind bars, even if, at least initially, for other crimes.

"Okay, so we're agreed on that, at least. Now, the small matter of liaison arrangements between the authorities in your country and ourselves. As you know, both James and our folks cannot be sure that Big Man's people in key positions back home won't seek to delay or even undermine our efforts here. O'Malley thinks that we should only send requests for information through official channels for stuff that may really be key to the case on the odd occasion; the rest should be decoys. What we really want to know we'll ask James through Mike here, and get the answers back the same way. So, here's the first: Could Big Man's chief of staff, — the guy you fellas got on tape in the hotel, can't remember his name now — but could he be put under discreet surveillance? Right now, he's one of two people who can directly link Big Man to the hit on Mike's family, and he's the only one not in custody."

Bassey looked puzzled. "Surely, there are three people, not two, who can link Big Man to the hit? As well as the Akin chap, both Casablanca and Morocco can link Big Man to the hit, surely?"

"Not Morocco. Winthrop will have his evidence ruled inadmissible on hearsay grounds, since he never heard Big Man give the orders. Casablanca, however, did, and Akin heard both of them discussing the hit. Besides, would you put

Morocco, an uncouth thug who can barely speak English on the stand in front of a Manhattan jury?"

"Point taken. If I know our boss, I would lay good money on the fact that Mr Akin can't scratch his balls, pick his nose or fart in bed without Mr Aloysius knowing about it in fairly short order, but doubtless Oga Mike here will pass the request on to Mr Aloysius."

"Certainly will." Mike said.

"Good. That, I think, is it, for now. Shall we convene again in three or four days?"

They all nodded. Holmes called for the bill, which he settled, and they made their way out into the parking lot. Adamu and Bassey were parked closest to the entrance and so got to their car first. Mike waved them off and turned to say goodbye to Holmes before heading towards his car. The FBI agent put his hand on Mike's arm to restrain him.

"Forget what I said in there about Morocco and Casablanca. What I really want you to tell James is to start working on a plan to get both Akin and Casablanca here to the States without anyone knowing about it. Tell him we're not going through the embassy on this one either, but we'll work directly with him to bring them in under the radar somewhere on the East Coast."

Mike was stunned. "But why?"

"Because I never trust anybody, my friend." Holmes smiled, nodded and walked away. It was only as Mike was in his car and headed back to New York that he realised that, by definition, Holmes' lack of trust must include him too. And, if James Aloysius was such a good pal of his, why didn't Holmes talk directly to him? Something did not add up here.

CHAPTER 13

Igore, Nigeria, five days later

THE DEED WAS ALMOST DONE. AS AKIN WATCHED on TV, the chairman of the Investigation Panel handed over a thick ring binder to the Speaker of the House of Assembly, both men looking suitably serious in a manner that belied the fact that the outcome of the whole charade was predetermined. The Speaker made all the usual noises about the House considering the findings of the Panel with an open mind, but everyone knew Big Man's days as governor were pretty much done. And with Big Man, Akin thought, went his own career in government. Well, he thought, things could be worse. He could not know that things were about to do just that.

The first indication was the entry into office of his secretary, who looked as if she'd seen a ghost. In a panicky voice, she said, "Sir, some people are outside to see you, they said they are from EFCC." She had barely got the words out when a young lady and a slightly older man entered on her heels.

"Mr Kazeem? My name is Miss Achu, and this is Mr Jegede. We're from the EFCC. Headquarters have instructed us to ask you to accompany us to Abuja to assist us with our enquiries into allegations of corruption and money laundering. Hopefully, it shouldn't take too long."

"Well, as you can see, things are rather busy here at the moment, so I doubt if it would be possible right now, maybe we could arrange—"

The man who'd been introduced as Mr Jegede interrupted

Akin. "Sir, we would rather this was done voluntarily, but please be in no doubt that we are prepared to formally arrest you if necessary."

Akin smiled wryly. "Put like that, how can I refuse?"

Keffi, Nigeria, the same day

Casablanca blinked as he emerged into the sunlight for the first time in several days. He lifted his handcuffed hands to shield his eyes from the dust thrown up by the swirling blades of the helicopter several yards away on the large field behind the detention centre that had been his home for the past several weeks. He barely had time to finish his breakfast of bean cakes and corn pap when the guards had come for him, slapped the handcuffs on him and hustled him out towards the helicopter, the sound of the arrival of which he had noted just before he was given his breakfast. After several weeks, he knew better than to ask what was happening; hopefully, the fact that he was being moved in broad daylight was a good rather than an ominous sign, plus this was the first time he was being taken anywhere by helicopter. Little did he realise he was about to undertake an even longer flight.

Nigerian Air Force Base, Kainji, Nigeria, later the same day

Both helicopters landed within minutes of each other at the far end of the runway. Any observers from the station buildings would have required binoculars to see that only one of the several people who disembarked from the helicopters was in handcuffs. They all entered a couple of buses and headed towards one of the hangars on the base. As the vehicles approached, the hangar doors opened to reveal a small white jet aeroplane with a Panamanian registration number on its fuselage and no other markings. Slightly behind it and off to the right was another, slightly bigger jet, silver this time, with two thin blue lines running down its fuselage. At the foot of the stairs leading into the first aircraft stood two men in casual clothes, each one holding a clipboard. The bus in front pulled up by the stairs, and Casablanca was led out, still in handcuffs. One of the men waiting at the foot of the aircraft steps stepped forward and spoke briefly to his escorts, checking some details against the clipboard in his hand. Satisfied, he nodded and his colleague led Casablanca up the stairs and into the plane, still in handcuffs.

The second bus meanwhile drove past the hangar and towards a couple of black SUVs a few hundred yards away. As the bus approached the SUVs, Akin could see that they both had their engines running. He had been slightly surprised that the EFCC operatives who had come for him in his office earlier had driven with him towards the airport. He had assumed that he was being taken to the state headquarters of the agency, only to be told that their destination was the main headquarters in Abuja. He was even more surprised when, after a short flight in a helicopter and not a plane, they had come in to land at what, judging by the military aircraft he had spotted earlier, was probably the Air Force base in Kainji. His captors had declined to answer any of his questions, saying only that things would be explained to him shortly.

The bus pulled up behind one of the SUVs and Akin emerged into the heat. As he did so, one of the rear doors of the SUV opened, and one of his escorts beckoned him to enter. He did so, and immediately saw he was sitting next to a small, nondescript looking man.

"Good afternoon, Mr Kazeem, my name is James Aloysius. I am sorry that we are meeting in such a fashion, but I thought it was better for us to have this little chat away from prying eyes and ears. You are probably wondering why you are here. Let me explain. It has to do with the on-going trial in New York of your soon to be former boss. I am a policeman and I have been involved in this matter for some time now; I think you may have met a couple of people who work for me. Anyway, the FBI have requested that I ask you if you would be willing, if required, to give evidence in court regarding the conversation between your boss and his unsavoury thug, Casablanca, the one that occurred in the governor's office about the fatal attack on the Anako family. Please note that this is a request only at this stage; you are not under arrest, and you can decline to assist. You are in an entirely different position from Casablanca, who is under arrest, and is being extradited to the US as a material witness; in fact, I think that's him leaving now." He paused whilst the white jet emerged from the hangar, the deafening sound of its engines as it taxied and took off making conversation impossible. As the noise of the jet receded, he spoke again. "As I said, at this point, you are not under arrest. That, however, isn't quite the same as saying I do not have plenty of evidence upon which to arrest you, secure a conviction and send you to jail for a long time. I hope you will understand that my last statement was not an implied threat, just a statement of fact." Aloysius paused to let that sink in, and then resumed.

"I am authorised to say on behalf of the FBI that if you agree to travel to the US to assist them in their prosecution of your former boss, you will be treated as a guest of the US government, and will be free to return home whenever you want. I am also authorised to say that, in the event you consider it unwise to return to Nigeria after helping to secure the conviction and imprisonment of your former boss, the US government will look favourably upon an application for asylum, and will assist in relocating your family, and in settling you down. If, on the other hand, you decline, as you are fully entitled to do, you will be immediately returned to Igore as a free man ... for now. The investigation into your case will then proceed apace, and, I anticipate, come to a head pretty soon. After that, as they say, all bets are off."

Akin was by now sweating, despite the freezing cold air-conditioning in the car. He was under no illusions as to the fix he was in, the calmness of Aloysius' tone notwithstanding. Akin was not a fool, and realised that if he was in any way seen to be involved in helping the Americans convict and imprison Big Man, there could be no way he could return and live in Nigeria, at least not if he didn't have a death wish. If, on the other hand, he refused to play ball, he had no doubt that this small man sitting beside him would have absolutely no qualms about seeing to it that he was locked up for a very long time. It was a no-brainer, really.

"I can't say I'm eager to sample prison food. How's this going to work?"

Aloysius nodded. "A wise choice, if I may say so. Here's what's going to happen. You will shortly return to the aircraft that brought you here, and continue your journey to Abuja, where you will be formally arrested and interviewed for a day or two by the EFCC, after which you will be released on bail. In the meantime, news of your arrest will be leaked to the press, and the world will hear all about it. When you are in custody, you will telephone your wife, and ask her to apply for US visas for your family. The visas will be granted; shortly afterwards, they should book tickets to fly to Miami, for a holiday at Disneyland. Clear so far?" Akin nodded.

"Good. Once they are safely in the US, the arrangements for you to join them will be explained to you. I need to tell you now that it is unlikely that you will get to keep all of the assets you have acquired over the last few years, but don't worry, you won't be destitute. Any questions? No? Then I suggest you re-join your escorts for your flight to Abuja. Have a safe trip."

Brunswick Executive Airport, Maine, the next day

Randy P. Clark considered himself to be a patriot. He was proud of having served his country in the navy, and remained ready to defend and support those that helped to keep it safe. If that meant keeping the airfield open a little later than usual at the request of the FBI, in order to receive an aircraft carrying "Person(s) of National Security Interest", then that was exactly what he'd do.

New York, one day later

J. Henry Winthrop IV was in a hurry. He had attended a dinner at his local Rotary Club the previous night, where he had received an award for his service to the club. The wine had been good, and he had possibly had a bit too much, with the result that he had both overslept (and therefore running late) and had a slight hangover. Impeccably groomed as usual, he was not in the best of temper, and his mood was not improved by having his path blocked by what he assumed was a reporter seeking a quick sound bite.

"Mr Winthrop, how is your case involving the Nigerian governor going?"

Winthrop balefully eyed the lady with red hair and slightly overdone makeup. "Kindly step out of my way, ma'am, I need to get to work."

"Is it true that the prosecution's case against your client is stronger than it first seemed when the case began?"

Winthrop stepped off the sidewalk to bypass the reporter, but she walked along beside him. As she did so, she produced a manila envelope from her satchel and thrust it towards him. "I think you might find this material interesting for your defence."

Winthrop carried right on walking, making no attempt to accept the envelope from her. "I'd take it, if I were you. It's going to get out one day that you were offered this information, and how are you going to look when the world knows what you rejected?"

Winthrop paused and looked at her again. "Just who are you? You're not a reporter, are you?"

"Let's just say I am no friend of the government exceeding its powers. Do you want this or not?" She thrust the envelope towards him again.

She had Winthrop's attention now. "What's in it?"

"Only one way to find out."

United States District Court for the Southern District of New York, two hours later

"Your Honour, may Mr O'Malley and I approach the bench?"

The Honorable Carmella DiNunzio looked up from her notes and peered at Winthrop over her glasses. "Is this likely to take long?"

"Your Honour, that depends on you."

"Very well. I suggest that we meet in chambers. Members of the jury, please retire for a minute." The judge sat behind her desk, which was piled high with various books, files and papers. "So, gentlemen, what's this all about?"

"Your Honour, the defence has recently come into possession of some material that we regard as potentially important to the defence case, and we would like to request an adjournment to review this material with our client."

"Mr O'Malley?"

"Your Honour, I would need to be persuaded of the justification for interrupting the presentation of the government's case. Besides, if Mr Winthrop wishes to reconsider how the defence presents its case, he's at liberty to do so when the defence has its turn; I don't see why the government's case should be interrupted at this point, and for the reason he gives."

"Your Honour, as Mr O'Malley is fully aware, the defence is not under any obligation to rehearse its strategy with the government outside the court room. If, on the other hand, the defence is in any way unlawfully impeded in challenging the government's case incross examination, that would constitute grounds for seeking a mistrial."

There was a pregnant pause in the room, eventually broken by the judge. "How long do you need, Mr Winthrop?"

A few minutes later, Winthrop sat across a table in a small room in the court building from his client. The room had no windows and had a glass panel in its door, outside which sat a couple of federal marshals. Inside the room itself, the atmosphere was distinctly chilly, and that wasn't entirely due to the air-conditioning.

"Governor, we may have a problem. I was given some information on the way here this morning that could have a bearing on how we try this case. Do you know someone called Casablanca?"

Big Man looked slightly taken aback. "Who?"

"You heard me. He is apparently someone who did some, shall we say, slightly delicate work for you."

"Not really, if you're talking about who I think you mean. He was one of the local party chieftains, the sort of person one needs to deal with when running for state-wide office back home. Why?"

"You were apparently overheard discussing an attack on an opponent's family with him. The bad news is that both he, and the person who overheard you talking with him have given statements to the effect that you ordered the attack, and are willing to give evidence to that effect."

Big Man laughed derisively. "Absolute nonsense. And anyway, how are they going to give evidence if they're not here?"

"Think again, Governor. They are apparently in the U.S. and will be produced in court."

"And where, exactly, has this information come from?"

"As I said, it was handed to me on my way to court this

morning by a woman who seemed initially to be a reporter, although I have my doubts about that. And before you ask, I am having my people check out this woman and her information. If it's correct, we've got some hard choices to make."

"Like what?"

"If the information is correct, O'Malley has the option of, irrespective of the outcome of this trial, charging you with the homicide of at least one, possibly more, US citizens, committed in the course of the commission of another felony — that would count as an aggravating factor as far as capital punishment is concerned. With testimony from not just one, but two witnesses that can tie you to the allegation, it'll be a hard one to refute in front of a jury. I'd sooner avoid going down that route. I recommend strongly that, if our enquiries suggest this information is kosher, I approach O'Malley and seek to do a deal."

Big Man leaned forward and fixed Winthrop with a steely glare. "Absolutely not. Not now, not ever. Got that?"

Winthrop shrugged. "Your call. I'll update you when we hear anything new."

A few blocks away, the woman who had handed the envelope to Winthrop emerged from the ladies room in Macy's. You would have needed to have been either extremely bored or incredibly vigilant to have connected the early middle-aged woman with blonde, slightly greying hair with the red-haired younger woman who had entered the ladies a few minutes earlier. The red wig was at the bottom of one of the brown bags she carried in her left hand, and would soon be dumped in a trash can; the make up that had taken several years off her age had been removed and the cotton wool pads used to accomplish this flushed down the toilet. Exiting the store, she made her way back to Larry's Perfumes.

Brooklyn, New York, five days later

The rendezvous this time was a Thai restaurant in Brooklyn, so Mike arrived by taxi. He had booked the table in the name of Williams for a party of four, and was the first to arrive. He decided to go straight to the table, and persuaded the waitress to change the position of their table from one right at the front to another further back and off to one side. He ordered a beer and sat down to wait for his colleagues. As he did so, he reflected on events since their last meeting at the rib shack in Jersey several days earlier. As instructed, he had made contact with Mr Aloysius and passed on Mr Holmes' request regarding keeping Akin under surveillance. He had just begun to talk about Holmes' second and more furtive request when Aloysius cut him off, saying he would call right back. Mike was still pondering what this meant when his cell phone buzzed with an incoming call from a withheld number; he hadn't been particularly surprised to hear Aloysius' voice, albeit slightly distorted. He had passed on Holmes' request regarding covertly moving Casablanca and Akin to the US, which Aloysius had acknowledged and then hung up.

Mike was still unclear why Holmes hadn't communicated with Aloysius directly, if, indeed he didn't trust Bassey and Adamu; plus, if he didn't trust those two, why trust him, Mike? The only reasons Mike could think of were that he was in some way being tested, or that Holmes was worried about a possible compromise of the security of his communications with Aloysius. In any event, given what he'd seen so far of Adamu and Bassey, he would trust them with his life.

His reverie was interrupted by the arrival of those two gentlemen. "Evening, Sir, how are you? Good to see you again," Bassey said with a grin as he sat at the table. Adamu was a few steps behind him, having a word with the waitress—it seemed he was asking directions to the men's room as he headed past the table and across the room towards a side corridor which led to the washrooms, if the sign at the top of the wall was to be believed. Bassey asked the waitress for the same beer Mike was drinking and took an appreciative first sip.

"Good to see you too. What have you guys been up to?" "Usual stuff . . . liaising between Abuja and the FBI and prosecution team, sitting through interminable case progress reviews and waiting for the trial to resume. By the way, did you hear that Big Man has now been removed from office as the governor? The House apparently voted yesterday, by a large margin, to do so, and his erstwhile deputy was immediately sworn in. With friends like that, who needs enemies? Good thing is that this pause in the trial has enabled me to get away and see my family in Atlanta for a few days, which was really good."

"How are they doing?"

"Growing up fast. I'm really missing them, and I look forward to having them back home when Ekaette finishes her degree."

Adamu returned from the washroom and joined them at the table. "Evening Sir, good to see you again. I hope this ignoramus here hasn't been boring you too much?"

Bassey ignored him. Mike smiled at the banter and waved the waitress over to take Adamu's drink order. Just then Holmes arrived.

"Sorry I'm late, got delayed at the office with a meeting about another case that overran a bit. What are you all drinking? Beer? Great, I'll join you."

They soon ordered their food and chatted as they ate about all manner of things other than the case. The restaurant slowly filled up and the level of background noise slowly increased. Once their main courses had been cleared away, and coffee and liqueurs were ordered, Holmes leant forward.

"Guys, as you know, the case against our friend has been on hold at the request of the defence for a few days now.

Apparently, the defence has been made aware that there are a couple of witnesses who can directly link the defendant to the killing of a US citizen abroad, committed in pursuance of the felony offences for which the defendant is currently before the court—and that the aforesaid witnesses are not only now in the US, they are willing to give evidence against Big Man. I understand that the defence are in a bit of a funk, as they have not been able to find the source of the information, but their investigations have lead them to think that it may well be true. I understand, also, that they have been so far unable to persuade their client of the sense of negotiating some sort of a deal with the prosecution on the felony charges in return for the homicide charges being put on hold. What we don't know at this stage is what line the defence will take when the trial resumes in a couple of days, so we need to test out different war-game options and what our responses should be."

There was a brief silence as they digested what Holmes had just said. Eventually, Adamu spoke. "I presume these two witnesses are the same ones we spoke about last time? I presume also that there's no point asking how, or when they entered the US?"

Holmes nodded.

"Nor, I suppose, is there any point asking how the defence was made aware of all this?" Bassey chipped in.

"Well, actually, there is. Let's just say that a friendly reporter was happy to do the honours in return for an exclusive scoop when the whole thing is done and dusted," Holmes said with as straight a face as he could muster, which was pretty straight.

"So, the choice for Big Man is: plead guilty now to some of these charges and go to jail for some time, or play hardball now and run the risk of being found guilty, going to jail for a longer time AND run the risk of a capital murder trial later?" Adamu asked.

"Pretty much," Holmes confirmed.

Mike had been silent so far, listening to his colleagues, who had more experience in these matters. What they all lacked, however, was a personal interest in the outcome of the case, as well as first-hand knowledge of the defendant and one of the key witnesses. It was time to speak up. "He'll never agree to a deal in a million years. You have to understand that the ego of the man would never let him admit that he did wrong, that he is no better than a thief, which is how his public back home would see him, especially now that he has been impeached and removed from office. Plus, he is likely to retain some degree of confidence that, while he may not be able to directly get at the two witnesses, he retains enough clout back home to reach them indirectly, perhaps through threats to family and friends, and thereby undermine any homicide case against him. I think it would also be wise to remember that neither of the two aforesaid witnesses have a track record for being either paragons of virtue or of being particularly brave, and on both counts are likely to be vulnerable in the hands of a skilled cross-examiner."

Mike paused for a second. "One last thing. I'm the only person at this table who has a direct and personal interest in this matter. While I want that bastard behind bars for a longtime for what he has done to my family, I am opposed to capital punishment, and I don't think I could bring myself to support it, even against Big Man." He stopped and took a large gulp from his brandy glass.

There was another silence, broken this time by Holmes. "Thanks, Mike, I think that's a most helpful piece of insight. If you're right, then it seems the line we should take is to do our best to nail Big Man on the current charges, and keep our powder dry in terms of any potential trial on homicide charges in future; if that eventuality should arise, then the strategy should be not to seek the death penalty, right?"

Adamu nodded. "Makes sense to me." Mike and Bassey nodded in turn in response to Holmes' inquiring look.

"I will let O'Malley and his people know. Another round of brandy?"

Bassey beamed. "What a splendid idea."

Manhattan, New York, the next day

The conference room was much more luxuriously and tastefully furnished than the one in the office of the US attorney, but then, that was hardly surprising, given that these were the offices of Winthrop Associates. Along the oak panelled walls hung the portraits of J Henry Winthrop Senior, Junior and III, as well as sundry other Winthrops and partners over the firm's almost one hundred year history. The current J Henry Winthrop presided over this small meeting of a couple of lawyers and the firm's lead in-house investigator, as well as the former NYPD detective they sometimes employed for projects that prudence dictated the firm not be seen to be too directly involved with.

"So, what you got?" Winthrop barked at his investigators.

"You want the good news or the bad news?" Very few people in the firm could get away with speaking to Winthrop like that, but since the lead investigator had worked for the firm since the time of J Henry Winthrop III, and had been instrumental in making a few of J Henry Winthrop IV's youthful indiscretions *go away*, he could get away with it.

"What's the good news?"

"There isn't any. The bad news is that our enquiries have revealed that a *person of national security interest* (PNSI) was flown into a quiet airport in Maine a few days ago on a private aircraft from a company that the FBI and CIA often use; said PNSI, a black male, late 40s or early 50s was met by several FBI agents and taken away to an undisclosed location. There is no word regarding a second PNSI, but if that person was not in custody, or came voluntarily, they could have come in on a regular flight anywhere and without access to TSA records, we have no chance of finding that out. What we can, and have found out, is that both individuals appear to have made statements along the lines set out in the documents you were handed; if they both give evidence against your boy, he's pretty much all done."

"And the source?"

"A greater chance of finding a trace of the Yeti in Central Park than there is of her. If you ask me, I'd say this was that bastard O'Malley's way of throwing a cat amongst the pigeons in an utterly deniable way."

"Great. So, either I persuade our boy to see the sense of a deal now in exchange for some jail time, or run the risk of even longer time at the end of this case, worse still, a potential capital murder trial later. Got any more good news?"

"I told you, there ain't any. Besides, that's why you're the hotshot lawyer who gets paid the big bucks, right? You figure it out. If it cheers you up, if your boy is toast as you seem to think he is, the Feds will go after his assets following this trial; he won't have two dimes to rub together, let alone pay you to defend him in any murder trial. You might want to get him to think about that. Hope you got your fees for this one up front. Right. Was there anything else? If not, I'm outta here."

Winthrop waved his hand in dismissal, and the two investigators got up and left. Winthrop turned to the lawyers. "Anyone got any bright ideas?" The blank looks he got in return told him all he needed to know.

Metropolitan Correctional Centre, Manhattan, New York, later the same day

Winthrop liked this place less and less every time he visited it. He liked it even less because of the difficult meeting he was about to have with his client. He stood as Big Man entered the room. Winthrop couldn't help but notice that the man seemed physically diminished, undoubtedly as a result of enforced abstinence from booze and rich foods, but this only seemed to enhance his air of power and authority, which was quite a feat, given his current circumstances.

"Well?" he said as he sat down.

"I'm afraid it isn't great news. In short, it seems the information we were given is at largely accurate — someone matching Casablanca's description was surreptitiously flown into the US by a government agency, most likely the FBI, a couple of weeks ago. The statements that we were told that these witnesses have given appear to be as described. There is no sign of your other associate, and, finally, the woman who handed me the envelope appears to have disappeared into thin air."

"So what are you going to do about it?"

"Well, it's more like what YOU are going to do. Here's the situation as I see it. While we can try to rebut the government's case against you, it's unlikely that we can get all of it thrown out, so there is at least a 50-50 chance that the verdict will go against you. If we can kill the worst of the charges, it could significantly reduce any sentence you might get, but not as much as doing a deal with the government now would achieve — no, let me finish." Big Man had started to interrupt, but Winthrop was determined to have his say. "If the government are willing to do a deal, we will insist that the potential homicide charges, which could potentially be capital charges given the number of victims and the fact that two of them were children, be dropped. If you refuse to do a deal, you must understand that you could potentially end up on death row. In my view, where there's life, there's hope — we could, with luck, secure a pardon in a few years time, but not if you're on death row. I trust I'm making myself clear?"

Big Man smiled. It was not a particularly warm or friendly

smile. "Sure. Now let me make myself equally clear. There will be no deal, not now, not ever. I do not want to hear anymore about any deal. Are we quite clear on that?"

Winthrop shrugged. "On your head be it. I will need you to sign a document confirming that I have given you my professional advice in this matter and that you have declined to follow it." He pulled an envelope out from his briefcase and removed two sheets of paper out, which he slid across the table to his client. "Those are two identical copies, which I have already signed. Please sign both copies and one of them is yours to keep." After a perfunctory glance, Big Man scribbled on both and slid one back across the table to his lawyer. "Now can we get on with the job in hand?"

CHAPTER 14

United States District Court for the Southern District of New York, two weeks later

MIKE SAT AT THE END OF THE LAST BENCH IN THE row of benches reserved for the public. He looked around with interest, as this was the first time he had actually been in the room where Big Man was being tried. Mike arrived early, although he had been given an official pass by Holmes, which ensured easy and quick access. The room was starting to fill up because both sides had now rested and the final speeches to the jury were due to begin this morning. Winthrop's no-case submission at the end of the government's case had apparently been given very short shrift by the judge, and although he had then gone on to mount a spirited defence of Big Man, succeeding in undermining the credibility of quite a few of the documents upon which the government relied, the consensus of several observers and commentators was that the government's case remained pretty strong. Trouble was, the observers and commentators were not the people entrusted by law with making the decisions in this case, and God only knew what the jury made of the occasionally technical, and often tedious, documentary evidence they had been presented with. Besides, the final speeches by the government and the defence could still sway a few jurors, as could the judge's summing up. There was still a lot to play for.

Up front, Mike could see O'Malley and his team seated at the prosecution table, a few feet away from Winthrop and his people. Big Man had been brought in a few minutes earlier, and sat between Winthrop and one of his assistants. He looked trim and confident, as sharply dressed as Mike had always known him to be. Adamu and Bassey, as usual, were nowhere to be seen in the courtroom, although Mike was pretty sure they were somewhere in the building. He was aware that they were due to return to Nigeria once the final speeches were done; Mr Aloysius apparently needed them back to deal with the case of Casablanca's corrupt commissioner of police friend and a few others. Mike was still slightly uncomfortable about the whole business of the liaison between Holmes and Aloysius and the implication from the former that he didn't trust Adamu and Bassey, and perhaps even Mike himself. He was determined to thrash the whole thing out with Holmes before Adamu and Bassey left for Nigeria; perhaps their final meeting the following evening at an Italian restaurant in the Bronx would be a good opportunity to do so. But, first, there was the small matter of the closing speeches.

The court clerk announced in a pompous voice the impending arrival of the judge, and everyone stood. Judge DiNunzio entered and took her seat. Having settled herself, the clerk announced that the court's business was about to begin, after which everyone sat down. The judge peered owlishly over the top of her glasses and asked both lawyers if they were ready to proceed. Receiving an affirmation from each of them that they were indeed ready with their final speeches, she asked the clerk to bring in the jury.

Mike looked with interest for the first time on the men and women in whose hands Big Man's fate lay. They were an eclectic collection—white, black, Hispanic, men, and women, fat, skinny, young and old. Mike idly wondered if they could truly be said to be a jury of Big Man's peers, but figured that since his peers were corrupt and greedy politicians, it was probably best that the jury were not Big Man's peers. Once the jury had settled into their seats, the judge nodded to O'Malley.

O'Malley got up and slowly walked over to the jury's box. He paused, looked at them without speaking for a moment, cleared his throat and began.

"Ladies and gentlemen, as you are aware, my principal job now is to summarise the case that the government has put forward over the past several weeks against this defendant, and to persuade you that that case has been made so that you are satisfied, beyond any reasonable doubt, of his guilt. That may be what the law says I now need to do, but, before I do that, I would like to thank you, on behalf of the government of the United States, for your time and patience in fulfilling your civic duty, upon which rests the foundation of the 'rule of law' by which this country is governed, and which has made our country the great nation that it undoubtedly is. We are a country of laws, and we take exception to those laws being violated with impunity. We particularly take exception when those laws are violated by those to whom we extend the hand of friendship, as we did to this defendant, by welcoming him to our country. In good faith, we welcomed him; he chose to repay our friendship by deliberately and wantonly seeking to put himself above the law. Ladies and gentlemen of the jury, I urge you to make clear by your verdict to this defendant, and others who may seek to emulate him, that in out country, nobody, and I repeat, nobody, is above the law." He paused for a couple of seconds to let this sink in. Over the next hour and a half, O'Malley clinically and dispassionately laid out the chain of evidence against Big Man, emphasizing each link in the chain by describing just how it constituted a violation of the law, and illustrating for the jury the consequences of Big Man's rapacious larceny by demonstrating just how many nurses and teachers salaries, how many doses of medication, or how many miles of road could have been delivered by the millions of dollars that Big Man had stolen—and had then had the temerity to try and launder through banks in the US. Mike thought that quite a few of the points O'Malley was making were of limited relevance to the case from a strictly legal point of view, but thought he could see what O'Malley was trying to do, which was to establish a wholly negative view of Big Man in the minds of the jury; from where he was sitting, Mike thought it was certainly making an impression on a few members of the jury, judging by the rapt attention they paid to O'Malley and the expressions on quite a few of their faces.

Just when Mike thought that the law of diminishing returns was starting to set in, O'Malley paused, glanced at his watch and then turned to address the Bench. "Your Honour, the next part of my address to the jury is likely to take some time, and I think it essential that I am able to address the jury without interruption; given the lateness of the hour, might this be a good time for the court to rise for the day? That way, all concerned can be fresh when the case resumes?"

It was very smoothly done, so smoothly done that the judge didn't even bother to ask Winthrop what he thought. "I think that's an excellent suggestion. The court will rise and resume at ten o'clock tomorrow." And that was that.

The Bronx, New York, later that day

Mike pushed away the plate of pasta carbonara that he had just demolished and sat back in his chair. "Good thing this trial is coming to an end . . . I'm not sure my waistline could survive another week of eating this kind of divine food."

"Sir, I am entirely with you on that front, although I have to confess that I can't wait to get home and have some ram *suya,* pounded yam and *edikang ikong* . . . in that order," Bassey said, sipping beer straight from the bottle. "How much longer do you think it'll be before the case goes to the jury?" Adamu asked.

"No later than tomorrow afternoon, might even be before lunch," Holmes speculated.

"Really? I thought Mr O'Malley still had a while to go, and then. . . " Adamu said, with some surprise.

"If I know O'Malley, that was just a stunt to make sure that the jury retired for the night with the negative impression of Big Man firmly implanted in their minds."

"Ah! A devious lot, these lawyers," Adamu said, nodding slowly.

"What time's your flight tomorrow?" Mike asked Bassey.

"22.45, I think. Mr OCD here can probably quote you chapter and verse on the flight, including the booking reference number, and the pilot's mother's maiden name" Bassey replied, jerking his head in Adamu's direction as he did so.

Adamu ignored him and turned to Mike. "I take it you're staying on till the verdict comes in, Sir?"

Mike nodded. "I have to see this through."

Holmes cleared his throat. "Guys, I would like to say that it has been a pleasure and a privilege to work with you. You've been fine ambassadors for your country in general, and for law enforcement in particular. I very much hope that our paths cross again, and—"

"Sorry to interrupt, but I need to clear something up with you," Mike fixed Holmes with a knowing look.

"I know, I know . . . I figured you'd want to do that at some stage," Holmes waved a resigned hand.

Adamu and Bassey exchanged slightly puzzled looks. Holmes looked at them and sighed. "Remember when we met at the rib place in Newark? I asked Mike to ask your boss to put the Akin chap under surveillance, right?"

Both Adamu and Bassey nodded.

"What you didn't know was that I asked Mike to tell James to get both Akin and Casablanca to the US under the radar, just in case. Why did I do it that way? Well, because James told me to. He also told me to create the impression in Mike's mind that he didn't fully trust you two. . . if you recall, Mike, what I said was that I didn't trust ANYONE, and you probably interpreted that to mean that I didn't trust your colleagues, but I suspected that it wouldn't take you long to figure out that 'anyone' included you as well, right?"

Mike nodded. "I figured that, but what I'm still not clear about is why? After all, I'm the one with a direct personal interest in this?"

Adamu looked at Bassey, and then, both of them burst into laughter.

Mike stared at them. "What's so fucking funny?" Eventually they were able to stifle their laughter.

"Sir, apologies, but you see, both Adamu and I know our boss a lot better than you do. If the thought crossed your mind that you were being tested, you thought right. Mr Aloysius was running the rule over you—I won't be surprised if you receive a call from him in the next few days inviting you to give him a call when you get back to Nigeria for a bit of a chat and a debrief. He clearly thinks a lot of you." Bassey said, still chuckling.

"Well, guys, I think y'all might have a few things to talk about amongst yourselves, so I think I'll leave you all to it. And don't worry about the check, it's taken care of. See you tomorrow." And with a wave, Holmes was gone.

Mike turned to the other two. "I think you two smug bastards have got a lot of explaining to do."

United States District Court for the Southern District of New York, the next day

Mike felt a little tender as he sat in court the next morning. The events of the previous night once Holmes had left were a little hazy in his memory, but as he slowly sobered up, more and more came back to mind. Adamu and Bassey had been initially incredibly vague as to what, exactly, it was they did, but eventually he managed to prise some information out of them—they apparently worked directly for Aloysius in a small unit that was dedicated to fighting corruption within the police, but beyond that, he had been unable to get them to disclose any specifics—apparently, Aloysius himself would more than likely fill Mike in on whatever he wanted him to know. The three of them had then gone on a bender of impressive proportions, with Bassey, as usual, in the lead, but even Adamu had let his hair down for a change; as Mike discovered, Adamu was a talented mimic with a surprisingly blue sense of humour. It was approaching 4 a.m. when Mike had been dropped off in a taxi at his hotel by the other two; he'd barely made it to court in time for the 10 a.m. start.

As Holmes had predicted, O'Malley finished his address to the jury within ten minutes of resumption, and now Winthrop was on his feet.

"Ladies and gentlemen of the jury, you have heard the government's case against my client, and if you perhaps thought you were listening to the sales pitch of a snake-oil salesman, you might be forgiven, for in my experience, rarely has a case been put before a jury that has been thinner than the soup made from boiling the shadow of a mosquito with anorexia than this one has been. The simple truth of the matter is that all my client has done is to seek to improve the lot of his people by establishing an industry that would provide employment for them, to enable them put food on the table for their families, and all the other things that a responsible government wants for those that elect them to power. No reasonable person could possibly take exception to that, but, as we have seen, sometimes the government of our country, acting in your name and mine, does not always do so with reason. At the very best, all the government has done is to demonstrate that good people, acting with the best of intentions, are not immune from being scammed by fraudsters and charlatans—but, the last time I looked, being the victim of fraud is not a felony in the United States.

"Where, you may ask, is the evidence? The answer, plain and simple, is: there isn't any. The government produces documents signed by more than one party, but fails to produce the parties other than the defendant; it produces audio recordings which allegedly involve my client, but fails to produce the other parties; it avers that the object of a completely legitimate business venture is to launder the proceeds of crime, but fails miserably to demonstrate that any crime has occurred.

The government would have you believe they are grateful to you for your time in listening to the fables they have presented to you, allegedly dressed up as evidence; what, in fact, they should have done was to apologise to you for wasting your time in making you listen to a poorly concocted set of fairy tales that would not convince a four year old child, never mind a jury of sensible adults such as yourselves.

"It may surprise you to learn that on one thing, Mr O'Malley and I agree, and that is that we are a nation of laws; laws, ladies and gentlemen, not fairy tales. Unlike him, however, I am utterly confident that you are more than able to tell the difference, and reach the only verdict possible, which is to acquit the defendant, and return him to his own country where he can resume doing the work of serving his people. Thank you very much for your attention."

Winthrop returned to his table and resumed his seat beside Big Man, who reached across and patted his lawyer on the forearm with approval.

Judge Di Nunzio then spoke. "Ladies and gentlemen of the jury, you have heard all the evidence in this case, and heard the final arguments of the government and the defense. What you are about to hear from me is a summary of the law that applies and is relevant in this case; what I am about to tell you is the basis, and the only basis, upon which you will weigh the evidence you have heard and reach a verdict having done so. So please listen very carefully."

JFK International Airport, New York, later that evening

Bassey looked at Adamu with some exasperation. "How come you don't seem to look or feel like any other normal human being would do after a night like last night?"

Adamu smiled broadly at him. "Because, unlike some people, I had the sense to drink only water after 1 a.m. . . . wasn't referring to you, Sir," he added hastily, this last directed at Mike.

"Don't worry, I fully deserve it," Mike replied with a wry smile.

The three men were sitting in a bar, each of them with a large glass of water with ice, a consequence of the previous night's excesses. Mike was there to see off the other two, who were heading back to Nigeria. It had suddenly dawned on him earlier that afternoon how much he had come to like, respect and admire them, and, while he had a vague recollection of having said so to them in the course of the previous night, he felt he needed to do so again when they were all more sober. He had managed to catch them before they left for the airport, and had insisted on seeing them off.

"Gentlemen, I really can't remember whether I said this last night or not, but I just wanted to let you know how very deeply grateful I am for all your help in trying to nail Big Man for what he did to my family. I could never have done it on my own, and whatever happens now, I want you to know that you will always have a friend in me forever."

The other two shifted uneasily in their seats, looking vaguely embarrassed. For once, Bassey didn't have a wisecrack retort, and eventually Adamu spoke up. "Sir, it was our duty and pleasure to help. So, what next for you now?"

"Funny you should ask, I was just thinking that I need to get back to work soon. I'm going to stop being paid by OP3 at the end of this month, and while I can keep going for a while longer, I do need to start earning again soon."

"Well, Sir, I wouldn't have thought that would be a problem for someone as talented and well-qualified as you," Bassey said. "Do you think you'll stay in Nigeria or head back to the UK?"

"Not sure that either really appeal to me right now, to be honest. I will come back to Nigeria initially, if only because I need to tidy up my affairs and, hopefully report to Ronke's parents that the bastards who were behind the deaths of their only daughter and grand children are behind bars. Talking of which, what's happened to Casablanca and Morocco? Or Akin for that matter?"

Bassey's face had a look of innocence on it that a choirboy would have been very proud of indeed. "No idea, Sir. I suspect we'll find out depending on the outcome of the current trial. If Big Man goes down for a long time, the Americans may be content with that, and not bother with a murder trial. Hard to say right now."

"I think we need to make a move Sir — you know how long-winded and precious security has become at airports these days. We don't want to miss our flight, do we now, young man?" Adamu said, nudging Bassey with his elbow. "Listen, my friend, I'm three whole months older than you, and don't you ever forget it," Bassey replied, but stood up all the same. He stuck out his hand. "Please let us know when you're back in Abuja, it would be great to catch up."

Mike knocked aside the proffered hand and gave both men a big hug in turn. "Will do. Have a safe trip guys, and please do me one last, big, favour — my name's Mike, not Sir."

"Absolutely, Sir!" both men said in unison, with big grins.

CHAPTER 15

United States District Court for the Southern District of New York, six days later

AS MIKE STEPPED OUT OF THE SHOWER IN THE GYM, he saw that he had a text message from Holmes. The jury had convicted Big Man on both counts of the indictment after two days of deliberations and Judge DiNunzio had now apparently sent word to both sides that the sentencing hearing would commence in a week's time. As Mike munched a late breakfast, he tried to make sense of the thoughts and emotions swirling around his mind. Would the Americans have the stomach for another courtroom fight on murder charges? Would he? What was he going to do next with his life? Well, he thought, things would soon start becoming clearer.

Mike watched as the US Marshals brought Big Man into Court. Now that he had been convicted, gone were the sharp suits; instead, he was dressed in jail issue navy blue trousers and light blue striped shirt. On his feet he wore a cheap pair of trainers. And the old swagger was definitely gone, replaced by an air of disbelieving resignation. He held his hands out for the marshals to remove the handcuffs around his wrists, and once they were off, he took a seat at the table beside Winthrop. They spoke briefly and quietly to each other, then stood and turned their attention to the bench as Judge DiNunzio entered and took her place.

"Are we good to go, gentlemen?" she said as she sat down.

Winthrop and O'Malley glanced at each other for a second,

then both nodded, and O'Malley answered for the both of them.

"Your Honour, we are."

"Fine. Let's get started, shall we?"

O'Malley stood up slowly. He rearranged a few papers and then looked up at the Bench. "Your Honour, as the government made clear in the course of the trial, we strongly believe that the defendant laundered several million dollars through U.S. banks; we also believe that those funds represented the proceeds of corruption, and that, therefore, the offences for which he appears before this court today for sentencing flow from other crimes which would be regarded as felonies within this jurisdiction. The jury, in convicting him, have clearly signalled that they were persuaded beyond a reasonable doubt of the truth and validity of the government's case. Your Honour will not need me to remind her that the commission of one felony in the course of the commission of another represents an aggravating factor to be taken account of in sentencing, as does the sum of money involved. It is the government's view that the crimes that the defendant has been convicted of are of a sufficiently serious nature that a sentence of imprisonment is inevitable; we are also of the view that such a sentence needs to be a lengthy one in order to serve the ends of justice, retribution, and a deterrent to others. Beyond that, Your Honour, the government has no further comments to make at this time, save that it reserves the right to arraign the defendant on further felony charges, the nature of which I believe are known to Mr Winthrop and the defendant."

Judge DiNunzio peered at O'Malley over the top of her glasses with a look that suggested she might have just stepped on dog poo on the pavement. "Mr O'Malley, your last comment could be misinterpreted by another judge as representing some form of improperly seeking to influence the court in the exercise of its discretionary powers over sentencing . . . before I do so, I invite you to withdraw it."

"Your Honour, I apologise if I inadvertently created such an impression. I of course withdraw the offending statement in its entirety."

"Good." She then turned attention to Mr Winthrop.

Winthrop rose. "Your Honour, thank you. I would urge you, on behalf of my client, to consider his current plight. You see before you today a broken man. Only a matter of a few weeks ago, he was a state governor, having been elected to that office by his fellow citizens. Prior to that, he had served his people for several years in several different capacities, including serving in the cabinet at both state and federal level. He of course accepts that he has been convicted after a jury trial, and that he must now reconcile himself to his fate, which lies in your hands, Your Honour. He does ask, and I ask on his behalf, that Your Honour take into account his years of sterling service to his people, and the fact that, prior to this current matter, he had never been arrested, never mind convicted of even the slightest misdemeanour; he is therefore someone of previous unblemished character, which as Your Honour will be aware, is clearly a mitigating factor in your consideration of sentence. Finally, I would ask that the court temper justice with mercy. . . for as the Good Book reminds us, we have all sinned, and fallen short of the glory of God."

"Thanks for the sermon, Mr Winthrop. Impressive, if not wholly relevant to the matter at hand. Will the defendant please stand?"

Big Man rose, and Winthrop rose with him. The judge fixed him with an inscrutable look. Big Man returned it with interest.

"You have been convicted, in my view rightly and on the basis of some very compelling evidence, of two serious felonies, involving the laundering of what I am satisfied are the proceeds of crime through the U.S. banking system. The funds involved run into several million dollars, monies that rightfully belong to the people of your country who, unwisely as it turned out, trusted you to lead them. I am required, in passing sentence, to weigh aggravating and mitigating factors in the balance. I accept that you are a man with no previous convictions; Mr Winthrop, on your behalf, invites me to therefore regard you as a man of previous unblemished character. I regret that I must decline his invitation—the absence of previous convictions is not necessarily synonymous with the presence of good character, and may represent nothing more than you have had the good fortune of not having been caught and held to account before now. On the other hand, I am satisfied that these current offences involved, by any measure, large sums of money, and were committed in the context of other criminal offences, namely corrupt enrichment, albeit in the absence of a formal conviction. I note also that you had the opportunity to plead guilty to these offences, and declined to do so, which of course you are entitled to do. On balance therefore, it is my view that the aggravating factors in this case outweigh the mitigating ones."

Judge DiNunzio paused for breath, then continued. "It is the sentence of this court that on each of the counts of the indictment upon which you have been convicted, you will serve a sentence of 14 years imprisonment, the sentences to run concurrently. I also order that the funds involved in this matter be forfeited to the government of the United States; it is, of course, open to the government of your country to seek the return of those funds to the people of your country. That's all."

The judge rose, as did everyone else in court. As she left the Bench, the marshals were handcuffing Big Man again. As he was being led away, he turned and looked straight at Mike, a look full of rage and hatred. Mike stared straight back at him, but found himself shivering involuntarily. And then Big Man was gone.

A few minutes later, Mike stood at the entrance to the court, watching as Winthrop announced to the waiting press that his client would be lodging an appeal against the verdict of the court. He felt a presence at his elbow and turned to see Holmes. They both stood in silence for a while, then Holmes spoke. "I thought he would get longer than that, but I suppose 14 years isn't too bad."

"Do you think O'Malley will pursue the homicide charges now?"

"No idea, but I would, if I were in his shoes."

Mike was silent for a minute. "Well, I suppose we'll find out soon enough. I just hope he doesn't opt to seek the death penalty, because, as I said, I'm not sure I could bring myself to be involved with that, even for such an odious reptile as Big Man." He turned to Holmes and held out his hand. "Thank you very much for all your help, I really do appreciate it."

Holmes grasped the proffered hand firmly. "My pleasure, glad to have been of help. You heading back home now?"

"I think so, just as soon as I can sort out a flight. I have some unfinished business with my parents-in-law."

EPILOGUE

Ijebu-Ode, Nigeria, one week later

THE HOUSE WAS JUST AS HE REMEMBERED IT — RONKE's Dad's study still as untidy as ever, the classical music still playing in the background, the stash of fine brandy under the desk, Ronke's mum fussing about feeding everybody properly. He realised as soon as he walked in how much he had come to love his parents-in-law, and how much he missed his own family. He had broken down in tears as soon as his mother-in-law enveloped him in a huge hug, and it seemed all he had done since his arrival the previous day was laugh and cry alternately as he and Ronke's parents recalled different things about Ronke and the twins. He hadn't realised the burden of grief he'd been carrying around, and it just seemed right that it was with Ronke's parents that he had been able to unburden himself of that grief.

And now, with another glass of his father-in-law's superb cognac in his hand, he was telling them both about the events leading up to the trial in New York — well, at least some of it. "So, in a nutshell, what they had in mind was to scare me off making the wrong decision, as they saw it, on the Ports privatisation project. I'm afraid Ronke and the twins were in the wrong car that day, and the goons that Big Man's henchmen sent panicked and exceeded their orders. The charges about the attack on Ronke and the kids remain outstanding, and the Americans should confirm in the next few weeks whether or not they're going to proceed — I suspect that they probably will, especially since the FBI's view is that Big Man got off lightly on the money laundering charges. You should know, however, that I've told them that if they do proceed and seek the death penalty, they can count me out of being involved."

Ronke's mum dabbed at her eyes for the umpteenth time. "Killing him isn't going to bring them back, is it? I just want him to rot in prison for the rest of his life for what he did, and that's more likely to happen over there than here, *abi*?

"Yes Ma," Mike replied. There was silence for a while. Mike noticed that his father-in-law hadn't spoken much. "Prof, you've not said much."

"What do you want me to say? Personally, I would kill that bastard myself, but the pair of you won't agree, I know. You better make sure they proceed with the murder charges, otherwise the U.S. Embassy and Department of Justice will hear from me." He took another sip of his brandy, then looked at Mike. "So what are you going to do with yourself now?"

Mike shifted uneasily in his chair. "Not entirely sure yet, to be honest. I have to go to Abuja to tie up some loose ends, then I was thinking about possibly looking at some job opportunities in the Middle East; to be frank, I think I've had enough of Nigeria right now, and I'm not keen on going back to the UK either."

Ronke's Mum sighed. "You know you're the only family we have left now."

Abuja, Nigeria, three days later

Mike stared at James Aloysius with some incredulity. "You want me to do what?"

Aloysius looked at him with no expression on his face and repeated himself patiently and slowly, as if speaking to an idiot child. "I want you to consider coming to work for me."

"But why? As far as I know, you're some sort of policeman, which I am most definitely not, so what on earth makes you think . . ."

"Okay, let me tell you," Aloysius interrupted him. "These two friends of yours," he said, jerking his head in the direction of Adamu and Bassey, who were doing their best to look anywhere but at him "are part of a very small, very discreet task force whose remit is to detect and prosecute corruption within the police. That remit has just been broadened to include all the security and intelligence agencies, and is being transferred from the control of the Inspector General of Police to that of the National Security Adviser. That means we need more people, with the right skills, and several things about your involvement with the whole Big Man thing impressed me."

He held up a hand and started ticking off the points on his fingers. "For one, you showed that you were able to divorce your personal emotions from the job at hand. Second, you can think outside the box. Three, you're persistent and don't give up. Four, you know how to keep your mouth shut. Five, you strike me as a man of integrity. And finally, you worked well with these two clowns."

Mike turned slightly and looked at Adamu and Bassey. "Did you guys know about this?"

"No Sir. Mr Aloysius doesn't always take us into his confidence," Bassey replied, looking slightly pained.

Adamu seemed to be finding his fingernails intensely fascinating. Mike turned back and looked at Aloysius, who looked placidly back at him.

"Well?"

Mike stared at him. "Do you really think I'd be any good at this?"

"Yes. And you know why?" Mike shook his head. "Because you understand that revenge is a dish best served cold."

Lightning Source UK Ltd.
Milton Keynes UK
UKHW02f0943140218
317868UK00009B/153/P